THE RACE FOR LOVE

Clint Wilbur was standing quietly in the Drawing-Room in front of the fireplace. Alita stood only a few feet away.

"You are well?"

"Of . . . course."

The words they were speaking did not really matter. Something magnetic like a spark of fire ran between them.

"Wh . . . *why* have you come . . . here?" Alita whispered.

"I could not wait any longer. I had to see you!"

He took a step forward and put his arms around her. As his lips sought hers she seemed to melt against him. Suddenly, he was kissing her fiercely, passionately.

He kissed her until the walls of the Drawing-Room swung round her. Until there was music in her ears. Until they were no longer two people but one and she was a part of him.

When finally he raised his head Alita could only look at him and say what was in her heart:

"I love . . . you!"

Bantam Books by Barbara Cartland
Ask your bookseller for the books you have missed

1 THE DARING DECEPTION
4 LESSONS IN LOVE
6 THE BORED BRIDEGROOM
8 THE DANGEROUS DANDY
10 THE WICKED MARQUIS
11 THE CASTLE OF FEAR
22 A VERY NAUGHTY ANGEL
24 THE DEVIL IN LOVE
25 AS EAGLES FLY
27 SAY YES, SAMANTHA
28 THE CRUEL COUNT
29 THE MASK OF LOVE
30 FIRE ON THE SNOW
44 THE WILD CRY OF LOVE
45 THE BLUE-EYED WITCH
46 THE INCREDIBLE HONEYMOON
47 A DREAM FROM THE NIGHT
48 CONQUERED BY LOVE
49 NEVER LAUGH AT LOVE
50 THE SECRET OF THE GLEN
52 HUNGRY FOR LOVE
54 THE DREAM AND THE GLORY
55 THE TAMING OF LADY LORINDA
57 VOTE FOR LOVE
61 A RHAPSODY OF LOVE
62 THE MARQUIS WHO HATED WOMEN
63 LOOK, LISTEN AND LOVE
64 A DUEL WITH DESTINY
65 THE CURSE OF THE CLAN
66 PUNISHMENT OF A VIXEN
67 THE OUTRAGEOUS LADY
68 A TOUCH OF LOVE
69 THE DRAGON AND THE PEARL
70 THE LOVE PIRATE
71 THE TEMPTATION OF TORILLA
72 LOVE AND THE LOATHSOME LEOPARD
73 THE NAKED BATTLE
74 THE HELL-CAT AND THE KING
75 NO ESCAPE FROM LOVE
76 THE CASTLE MADE FOR LOVE
77 THE SIGN OF LOVE
78 THE SAINT AND THE SINNER
79 A FUGITIVE FROM LOVE
80 THE TWISTS AND TURNS OF LOVE
81 THE PROBLEMS OF LOVE
82 LOVE LEAVES AT MIDNIGHT
83 MAGIC OR MIRAGE
84 LOVE LOCKED IN
85 LORD RAVENSCAR'S REVENGE
86 THE WILD, UNWILLING WIFE
87 LOVE, LORDS AND LADY-BIRDS
88 A RUNAWAY STAR
89 THE PASSION AND THE FLOWER
90 A PRINCESS IN DISTRESS
91 THE JUDGMENT OF LOVE
92 THE RACE FOR LOVE

Barbara Cartland's Library of Love series

- 3 THE KNAVE OF DIAMONDS
- 4 A SAFETY MATCH
- 6 THE REASON WHY
- 7 THE WAY OF AN EAGLE
- 8 THE VICISSITUDES OF EVANGELINE
- 9 THE BARS OF IRON
- 10 MAN AND MAID
- 11 THE SONS OF THE SHEIK
- 12 SIX DAYS
- 14 THE GREAT MOMENT
- 15 GREATHEART
- 16 THE BROAD HIGHWAY
- 17 THE SEQUENCE
- 19 ASHES OF DESIRE
- 20 THE PRICE OF THINGS
- 21 TETHERSTONES
- 22 THE AMATEUR GENTLEMAN
- 23 HIS OFFICIAL FIANCEE
- 24 THE LION TAMER
- 25 IT

Barbara Cartland's Ancient Wisdom series

- 1 THE FORGOTTEN CITY
- 2 THE HOUSE OF FULFILLMENT
- 3 THE ROMANCE OF TWO WORLDS
- 4 BLACK LIGHT

Barbara Cartland
The Race for Love

THE RACE FOR LOVE
A Bantam Book / October 1978

*All rights reserved.
Copyright © 1978 by Barbara Cartland.
This book may not be reproduced in whole or in part, by
mimeograph or any other means, without permission.
For information address: Bantam Books, Inc.*

ISBN 0-553-12292-4

Printed simultaneously in the United States and Canada

Bantam Books are published by Bantam Books, Inc. Its trademark, consisting of the words "Bantam Books" and the portrayal of a bantam, is registered in the United States Patent Office and in other countries. Marca Registrada. Bantam Books, Inc., 666 Fifth Avenue, New York, New York 10019.

PRINTED IN THE UNITED STATES OF AMERICA

Author's Note

In 1890, five years after the setting of this novel, Lieutenant-Colonel Sir William Gordon Cumming, a close friend of the Prince of Wales was detected cheating at baccarat at a house-party at Tranby Croft in Yorkshire.

Accused by other guests, Sir William signed a document never to play cards again, in consideration of all those gentlemen present, and to "preserve silence" as to what they thought had occurred.

But gossip spread even to Paris, and Gordon Cumming threatened to bring an action for slander against his original accusers.

However, when he asked leave to retire from the Army, the Adjutant General rejected his application and ordered him to appear before a Military Court.

In due course not only most of the distinguished guests at the house-party were subpoenaed to give evidence at the trial but also the Prince of Wales.

Although Sir William always protested his innocence and his leading Counsel believed whole-heartedly in him, the Lord Chief Justice made a strongly biased speech against him. The verdict was "guilty."

Dismissed from the Army, expelled from his

Clubs, boycotted by Society, Gordon Cumming once said to his daughter:

"Among a host of acquaintances I thought I had perhaps twenty friends, but not one of them ever spoke to me again."

The Shows at the Gaiety Theatre at the end of the century gradually ceased to be Musical Burlesque and became Musical Comedy. *Little Jack Sheppard* was a smash hit, with Nellie Farren in the title lead and Miss Wadman also playing a male part.

Chapter One

1885

The Duke walked into the Dining-Room and two of the ladies having breakfast hastily rose to their feet.

"Good-morning, Hermione!" he said, his eyes resting for a moment with appreciation on his daughter's pink-and-white beauty.

"Good-morning, Papa," Lady Hermione answered.

Without speaking the Duke glanced towards the girl who had risen from her seat at the other side of the table.

"Good-morning, Uncle Lionel!" she said quickly.

The Duke made no response, and with a sound curiously like a groan he sat down at the head of the table.

The Butler hurried to place in front of him on a silver stand a copy of *The Times*, which had been carefully ironed in the pantry.

A footman, having first filled his cup, set a pot of hot coffee in front of him, and another footman offered a crested silver dish.

"Sweetbreads again?" the Duke asked. "What else is there?"

"Kidneys, Your Grace, bacon and eggs, and salmon kedgeree."

The Duke reflected; then, with an expression on his face as if all of them were distasteful, he helped himself to the sweetbreads, which had been offered to him first.

"You must be tired, Lionel," the Duchess said in a solicitous voice; "the train was later last night than I have ever known it."

"The railway-service gets worse and worse!" the Duke said. "I had hoped to take a train that arrived earlier, but I was prevented from doing so."

"Prevented?" the Duchess questioned.

"That is something I intend to relate to you," the Duke said.

He spoke in a significant voice which his wife interpreted as meaning that he did not wish to speak until the servants had left the room.

The silver rack of hot toast was placed at his side and also a gold bell.

Then the Butler and the footmen withdrew, and as the door closed behind them, three pairs of expectant eyes were turned towards the head of the table.

The Duke was a good-looking man. He had been considered very handsome in his youth, but now his hair was turning grey and there were lines on his face which made him at times look older than he was.

However, he carried himself with a dignity and an air of consequence which made him outstanding wherever he appeared.

It was well known that Queen Victoria, who had a penchant for handsome men, liked the Duke to be in attendance upon her.

Although it necessitated many journeys to London, the Duke was nevertheless flattered that Her

Majesty frequently asked his advice and insisted on his presence at innumerable Court functions.

The Duchess had not weathered the years as well as her husband. She had been a pretty, fair-haired girl when the Duke married her, but now she looked somewhat faded, though this did not make her any the less a significant personality.

She had a presence which made strangers nervous and resulted in most of the parties which took place at Langstone Castle seeming very stiff and somewhat of an ordeal for those who took part in them for the first time.

Lady Hermione Lang was the pride of her father's heart. She was extremely pretty, with an unblemished English complexion, fair hair with touches of gold in it, and pale blue eyes the colour of a thrush's egg.

It was doubtful if she would have received so much attention and acclaim had she been born a nonentity, of no Social importance.

But, as she was a Duke's daughter, the glamour of her position added an aura to her looks which made those who saw her and read about her in the Society papers believe her to be more beautiful than she was in actual fact.

The other young occupant of the breakfast-table was very different.

Alita Lang was the Duke's niece.

She lived with her aunt and uncle under sufferance and she never appeared in what was known as the "front of the house" except when the family were alone.

While Lady Hermione was dressed in the very latest fashion, with a gown draped in the front and finished with elaborate embroidery which swept into a bustle at the back, Alita's gown was very different.

An extremely ugly shade of brown without any trimming, made by an obviously unskilled hand, it made her skin appear sallow and perhaps accounted for the manner in which her uncle looked at her disdainfully and quickly looked away again.

It was well known that the Duke had an eye for pretty women.

His wife could have related times of deep unhappiness when he had been fascinated by some charmer years younger than himself and she had found herself neglected at Balls, or ignored even in her own Drawing-Room.

Alita, however, was too used to the manner in which she was treated by her relatives for it to have any further power to hurt her.

And as if their attitude made her indifferent also to her looks, her hair was dragged back into an untidy bun at the back of her head.

She made no effort to prevent tendrils escaping from the confines of the pins and there were wisps trailing untidily on each side of her face.

The eyes with which she now looked at her uncle were grey, and they seemed to match her hair, which was an unusual colour. Someone had once described it as "ash."

"You are an ash-blonde," one of her Governesses had said.

But that was long ago in the past, when her appearance had been of importance not only to her father and mother but also to herself.

Now she seldom even bothered to look in the mirror in the morning when she rose, and if she did so when she changed for dinner it was merely to see that she did not look so unkempt as to evoke a reprimand from her aunt.

"What I have to tell you," the Duke said now with a slow pomposity which often infuriated his contemporaries, "is that Yeovil, who was poor D'Arcy's Trustee, kept me late at the Club discussing the sale of Marshfield House and Estate."

"It has been sold?" the Duchess exclaimed. "Then why did no-one tell me of it?"

"I am telling you now, my dear," the Duke said.

"I asked Mr. Bates only a week ago if they had heard of a purchaser," the Duchess went on in a complaining voice, "and he assured me that the house was too big to be interesting to many people. 'The Trustees are hoping they'll find a millionaire!' he said to me."

"And that is exactly what they have found!" the Duke remarked.

"A millionaire?"

"A multi-millionaire!" the Duke said firmly.

"Oh, Papa, that sounds exciting!" Hermione exclaimed.

"It is very exciting, Hermione," the Duke answered. "I was introduced to the gentleman in question two days ago at Windsor Castle by the American Ambassador."

"The American Ambassador?" the Duchess queried.

"The purchaser of Marshfield House, my dear, is an American!"

The Duchess looked obviously disconcerted, but before she could express her feelings the Duke went on:

"Clint Wilbur is, I assure you, a most personable young man. I have invited him for dinner tonight."

"Tonight?" the Duchess exclaimed, and it was almost a shriek. "But there is no time to arrange a party."

"We do not really need a party," the Duke said. "I thought it would be pleasant for Mr. Wilbur to meet us as a—family."

He looked at Hermione as he spoke, and the Duchess, who was not an obtuse woman, did not fail to understand what he was thinking.

"But an—American!" she said, as if he had spoken his thoughts aloud.

"The Wilburs, I understand, are a respected and distinguished family," the Duke said. "The Ambassador told me that they are related to the Vanderbilts and to the Astors."

"Is he really so rich, Papa?" Hermione enquired.

"I am informed that he is one of the richest and most eligible bachelors in America, and he owns an astronomical number of oil-fields, railroads, shipping-lines, and Heaven knows what else!"

As if the Duchess had finally got the message she said:

"We must certainly do our best to help Mr. Wilbur settle in. But why should he wish to buy such a large Estate in England?"

"That brings me to another piece of information," the Duke said in a tone of satisfaction. "Wilbur told me that he is interested in buying some horses, especially hunters. He will hunt with the Quexby."

Now the Duke looked at his niece, and as if he thought her attention was wandering he said sharply:

"Did you hear what I said, Alita?"

"Yes, Uncle Lionel."

"Then kindly see that the horses on which you spend so much time look their best when Mr. Wilbur comes to see them."

"I will do that, Uncle Lionel."

"I will discuss with Bates the prices we should ask for them."

"I have a much better idea of what they would fetch in a Sale-Room than Mr. Bates has," Alita said.

There was a momentary silence after she had spoken, as if the Duke resented her being so knowledgeable.

Then he replied grudgingly:

"Very well, I will discuss it with you. This is your chance to prove that the large amount of money you have inveigled me into spending on the stable has been worthwhile."

"I am sure Mr. Wilbur would find it difficult to find better horses to purchase, at least in this part of the country," Alita said.

"I hope you are right!" the Duke replied.

"Do not sell too many horses, Papa," Hermione pleaded petulantly. "I want some of your best ones to carry me out hunting this year. Those I rode last Season were far too wild. They frightened me!"

Alita looked across the table at her cousin and thought, as she had so often before, that it was really a mistake for Hermione to ride at all.

She was always afraid of her horse, however quiet it might be, and she looked far more attractive attending a Meet in a carriage or a pony-cart, and then driving home without taking part in the sport.

But Hermione was well aware that if she wanted to meet gentlemen without the stiff formality which existed in her parents' house, the best place was in the hunting-field.

Every winter, therefore, she forced herself to hunt with the fashionable Quexby fox-hounds, even though, as her cousin was well aware, she hated every minute of it.

"How many horses will Mr. Wilbur want?" the Duchess enquired.

"Let us hope he will buy the lot!" the Duke said. "God knows we need the money."

The Duchess sighed.

"I was going to speak to you on that subject, Lionel, but I decided to wait until you returned from Windsor."

"If you are about to ask me for an increase in your housekeeping allowance, or for any quite unnecessary decorations in the Castle, you can save your breath!" the Duke said.

He spoke sharply, and then turned his attention to *The Times*, opening it out with a great rustling of the pages and folding it neatly so that he could read, as he always did, the Editorial first.

"It is all very well, Lionel, for you to talk like that," the Duchess said plaintively, "but the curtains in the Drawing-Room are almost threadbare, and Hermione must have some new gowns this winter. She cannot appear at the Balls wearing the same clothes she wore last year."

Alita knew that once her aunt embarked on a list of the things she required for the house and her daughter, it would be an endless monologue.

Hastily she pushed back her chair.

"Will you please excuse me, Aunt Emily?" she asked. "After what Uncle Lionel has told us, I have a great deal to do."

"I will come down to the stables in about an hour's time," the Duke said. "Then we will discusss the prices of the animals we decide to sell."

"Very good, Uncle Lionel."

Alita went hastily from the room and the Duke remarked:

"That girl looks more like a scarecrow every day. Can you not tidy her up a bit?"

"What is the point?" the Duchess asked. "You know as well as I do that nobody sees her. But what I want to talk about, Lionel..."

She was off again on the familiar tack, and Alita, running down the corridor, was thankful that she had escaped.

She went up the staircase two steps at a time, and, rushing into her bed-room, threw off the gown she had worn for breakfast and put on her riding-habit.

It was very old, worn, and almost threadbare, but it had come from a very expensive tailor and the cut of it had not been lost in the years that it had been in service.

It looked very different on Alita from the shapeless, ugly gown which she had worn for breakfast.

She did not stop to look at herself in the mirror, but, having put on her riding-boots, she picked up her thin whip and once again ran down the corridor.

This time she took a back staircase which led her to the part of the Castle that was nearest to the stables.

It was a crisp autumn day, the leaves were still not off the trees, and the gardens contained a few late roses.

But Alita noticed nothing on her way to the stables, as she was deep in thought about the horses she loved.

She spent every moment of her time with them, when her aunt did not demand that she perform a number of household duties, which she found extremely tedious.

"Sam! Sam!" she called.

An old groom came from one of the stable-doors.

"What do you think His Grace has just told me, Sam?" Alita said in a lilting voice which she never used when she spoke to her relatives.

"Oi've no idea, Miss Alita!" Sam replied. "But it seems to a'pleased ye."

"Marshfield House has been sold!"

"Oi 'ears that!" Sam replied.

"You never told me!"

"Oi only 'ears it last night, Miss, down at th' *Green Duck*. They was a-saying as the new owner be a Amer-a-cane."

Sam pronounced the word in a funny way and Alita laughed as she said:

"He is a very rich one, Sam, and His Grace wants to sell him our horses. That means that if we can get a good price for them, we will be able to buy in to new blood-stock and perhaps purchase some outstanding mares."

"Oi 'opes as 'ow you're right, Miss," Sam said,

and his tone of voice sounded as if he doubted that such good fortune would come their way.

"Mr. Wilbur will be coming over any day," Alita said, "so we must make the horses look really impressive."

She paused before adding:

"I wonder if he knows anything about horses. I believe some Americans out in the West are good riders, but from what His Grace said about Mr. Wilbur, he sounds as if he is a business-man from New York."

"Oi thinks it's unloikely as 'e'll know one end of an 'orse from t'other!" Sam snapped.

"Which means that he will have no idea what they are worth," Alita said.

She glanced at the old groom and her eyes were shining.

"Come on, Sam! Let us go to work. If he is sufficiently dazzled by them, we ought to be able to get a good many of his dollars for them before he realises what has happened."

She did not wait for Sam to reply but hurried into the first stall that was open.

The stables at Langstone Castle had been built by the previous Duke, who had squandered a great deal of the family fortune on his horses.

His son, the present Duke, complained bitterly that if his father had spent the same sum in buying pictures or furniture, there would have been heirlooms to hand down to the next owner of the Castle, instead of horses, which lost their value all too quickly.

It was in his favour that the Duke, while trying to keep up appearances, was deeply concerned that his son Gerald would eventually inherit less than he had himself.

Her cousin Gerald, who was a Marquis, was presently in India, and Alita often told herself stories

THE RACE FOR LOVE

in which he accumulated a great deal of money there, as other people had done.

When he came home he could then spend it on filling the enormous stables with thoroughbreds, and then watch his horses carry the family-colours in the Classic races.

But when Gerald was away there was really no-one but herself to be interested in the horses they had bred.

When her uncle was in a disagreeable mood, Alita was aware, he grudged every penny that she and Sam must spend in keeping the stable fit and healthy if nothing more.

As she entered the long building she thought with satisfaction that they in fact owned some magnificent animals to show to Mr. Wilbur, or to anyone else who might be interested.

Sam was of course extremely short-handed, and if Alita had not worked as hard if not harder than any stable-boy, it would have been impossible for them to keep as many horses as they had at the moment.

The Duchess took it for granted that there would always be carriage-horses to carry her anywhere she wished to go in the country.

The animals were also taken to London for the Season to convey her and Hermione to Ranelagh and Hurlingham and to stand for hours waiting for them at night when they were attending some grand Ball.

The Duke had found that riding increased the pain he suffered from rheumatism and he had therefore left the hunting to Hermione and Alita.

The latter was well aware that she would not have been allowed to hunt even with an unfashionable pack if she had not been breaking in the horses which the Duke sold at a big profit as soon as she had brought them to the peak of perfection.

She had a perfect seat on a horse, light hands,

and remarkable expertise in training difficult animals.

It was a talent that the Duchess looked on as regrettable in a young woman.

But the Duke, who realised Alita's worth, turned a deaf ear to his wife's suggestion that she could be better employed sewing and running errands for her in the Castle.

"His Grace will be coming here within an hour, Sam, to discuss the prices we should ask. He wanted to talk it over with Mr. Bates!"

Sam chuckled.

"Ain't no use 'is Grace askin' 'im!"

"That is what I told him," Alita replied.

They both knew that Mr. Bates, the Agent, who had been at the Castle for over thirty years had long since given up interfering with anything to do with the stables.

He knew that Alita could better him in any argument about horses, and as he was getting old and tired he was only too grateful that one burden at any rate had been lifted from his shoulders.

"I suppose Double Star will be the American's first choice," Alita said as if she was talking to herself.

"Or Red Trump," Sam interjected.

"They are neither of them as good jumpers as King Hal," Alita remarked, "but for all we know he may be a gap-seeker!"

They both laughed, despising with the arrogance of experienced equestrians those who waited for a gate to be opened or looked for a gap in a fence.

When the Duke arrived in the stables it was to find Alita brushing down a horse and whistling as she did so in exactly the same manner as Sam was doing.

He frowned for a moment as he watched her, knowing that it was not the behaviour which was to be expected from a young lady.

Then he told himself that, as his wife had often said, Alita did not really come into that category.

It was of course through no fault of her own. At the same time, nothing could be done about it, and as long as she was useful to him it was really of no consequence how she behaved.

He must have stood watching her for a few seconds before Alita, who had been concentrating fiercely on what she was doing, looked up and saw him.

"Hello, Uncle Lionel!" she exclaimed. "I want you to look at Double Star. I think with a bit of luck we might get nearly five hundred guineas for him!"

"Make it a thousand!" the Duke said.

"A thousand?"

The Duke smiled.

"Mr. Wilbur can afford it."

"Yes, of course," Alita agreed. "At the same time..."

She stopped what she was saying and grinned at her uncle.

"Are you suggesting, Uncle Lionel, that we should sting him for everything we can get?"

"Those are not exactly the words in which I should have put it," the Duke said reprovingly. "I cannot think what your aunt would say if she heard you talking in such a manner—but briefly, the answer is 'yes'!"

Alita gave a little laugh.

When she and her uncle were alone together he forgot to be stiff and pompous and they talked without restriction, as if they were contemporaries.

"Very well, Uncle Lionel," she said. "I will do my best."

A quick frown came between the Duke's eyes.

"You suggest that you should negotiate with Wilbur yourself?"

Alita made a little gesture which was very eloquent, despite the fact that the brush was still in her hand.

"Who else?" she asked. "You know that old Sam would ramble on and never get to the point, and Mr. Bates would be far too honest to ask anything but the 'going price.'"

"Very well," the Duke agreed, "you shall talk to him."

"It will all be strictly business," Alita promised, "and of course he will not be aware that I am your niece."

"You are my brother's child," the Duke said heavily, "and nothing can alter that. There will be no question of this man being inquisitive about you, but, much as I regret it, you had better call yourself by another name."

Alita realised she had touched some pride in her uncle which she had suspected but had not actually known existed.

"Thank you, Uncle Lionel," she said softly. "I will be 'Miss Blair,' as I have been on other occasions."

Then in a different tone of voice she went on:

"Have a look at the others. It is a long time since you have seen them all together. I feel certain you will notice an improvement in their condition."

As the Duke walked from stall to stall he knew that Alita was right and there was an improvement.

He was honest enough to admit that to have raged at her for spending so much money, and sometimes to have categorically refused to spend more, had been a mistake.

She had always argued that as they had the stables, and as they also had the progeny from the original blood-stock on which the last Duke had spent a fortune, it was a mistake to waste it.

Now he was seeing that she had been right, and the results justified the expenditure even though he had often doubted it.

As they walked on, the Duke noted that although the stables were spotlessly clean and the horses comfortable, the cloths they wore were tattered and worn and the walls needed a fresh coat of whitewash.

As if she knew what he was thinking, Alita said:

"I have been meaning to do some decorating, but I just have not had the time."

The Duke put his hand on her shoulder.

"You have done more than anyone else could have done in the circumstances, my dear, and I am grateful. If you manage to bring off some good sales, I will see that you have a new gown as a reward."

"And when would I wear it?" Alita enquired.

There was a sudden silence, then the Duke's pressure on her shoulder increased and he turned away with a sigh.

'Why am I so foolish?' Alita silently asked herself when he had gone back to the house. 'He was trying to be kind. I should have accepted the gown and worn it to show the horses!'

She smiled at the thought, but there was a bitterness in the twist of her lips and in the expression in her eyes.

A moment later she was laughing and joking with Sam and then giving instructions to the three half-witted stable-boys who were all the help they could afford.

* * *

Clint Wilbur, who was riding over his newly acquired Park-land, appreciating the age of the great oaks and the beauty of the deer which scurried away at his approach, had a sudden idea.

He knew that tonight he was to dine with the Duke of Langstone, whose Estate marched with his own.

The Duke had spoken of his horses and Clint

Wilbur had decided it might be a good idea to have a look at them before they discussed the possibility of any purchase, perhaps after dinner.

Clint Wilbur was well aware that there were always people in the world who tried to extract money from him by one means or another.

He was surprised to find that the English lived up to their reputation as shop-keepers and were willing to conduct a sale at any moment of the day or night.

It was as if the mere thought of his millions made them reach out their hands towards his pockets.

He found that whether he was in the St. James's Street Clubs to which he had been introduced by some of the most important people in the land, or in the Ball-Rooms of the great hostesses, there was always at his elbow a seller of some commodity.

Because he was extremely intelligent and very shrewd, he disliked being thought of as a "sucker"! He therefore had no intention of being one, and took great care to prevent such an unlikely occurrence.

But he had seen the glint in the Duke's eye when he had talked about his horses; and he was quite certain that, after the port had passed round the table a considerable number of times, after dinner the subject would come up.

'I will have a quick look at them,' Clint Wilbur thought to himself, 'and if they are no good I will make it quite clear that I already have all the horses I require and am not in the market for any more.'

It was not difficult for him to know in which direction the Castle lay, because, being built on high ground, and with the Tower with the Duke's flag surmounting it, it could be seen from many different parts of the Marshfield Estate.

Clint Wilbur now rode towards it, taking his route as the crow flies, and soon after he had crossed from his own property into the Duke's he came to what he saw at a glance was no less than a race-course.

It had in fact been laid out by the late Duke, and Alita had spent a great deal of time, with the help of some village yokels, in reconstructing the jumps.

The race-course was quite a large one, as the old Duke never did anything by halves.

Just as he poured out money in an inexhaustible stream on anything that concerned his horses, the race-course had been planned by experts in the most expensive manner.

Clint Wilbur drew his horse to a standstill and looked at it appreciatively, wondering if he might impose on his neighbour's generosity and try some of the fences himself.

Then as he thought of it he saw that there was already someone doing that very thing.

As the horse and rider were at the far end of the course, he did not realise until they approached much nearer that there was a woman in the saddle.

She was taking the very high jumps in a manner which Clint Wilbur knew was an exceptional feat of riding.

As she drew nearer he saw that she was encouraging her horse and taking him over the fences with an expertise that was remarkable, and talking to him as she did so.

The jump a little to the right of where Clint Wilbur stood was a very high one with a ditch on the other side of it.

Just as they reached it, the horse, and he saw that it was a young one, refused.

There was nothing rough in the way he was treated. The woman riding him bent forward to pat his neck, spoke to him encouragingly, then turned him round and took him at the jump again.

This time she seemed almost to lift him over it

by sheer will-power, and when he cleared it without touching a twig of the fence she patted him; and Clint Wilbur heard her say:

"That was splendid! Clever boy! Now, shall we go back and do it again?"

Before she could turn round, Clint Wilbur urged his own horse forward.

He saw that as the woman became aware of him there was a startled expression on her face.

She was wearing an old tattered jockey-cap pulled low over her forehead, and the white shirt under her riding-habit was undone at the neck.

"Good-morning!" Clint Wilbur said. "May I say how much I admire the manner in which you are riding that horse?"

"Thank you," Alita answered.

She thought as soon as she saw him that this must be their new neighbour. Besides, she had never seen anybody who looked quite like him.

It was obvious as soon as he spoke that he had a faint accent.

It was surprisingly faint and yet it was there, and she thought he was very different from what she had imagined he would be like.

Somehow she had always thought that Americans were small men, but the man facing her was well over six feet tall, handsome, well proportioned, and she guessed athletic.

His eyes were blue, and his bronzed, sun-burnt face made them appear more vivid than they actually were.

But what intrigued her was the fact that he sat his horse in the manner which she knew acclaimed him as a rider of undoubted ability and someone who had obviously spent a great deal of his life in the saddle.

As if he was amused by her scrutiny Clint Wilbur asked:

"I would like your permission to join you and see if I can take these fences as well as you have done."

Alita looked not at him but at the horse he was riding.

"May I suggest that you try them first on one of our horses which have been over them a number of times? There are three of them waiting down there."

She pointed to the other end of the race-course, and as if he accepted the suggestion without unnecessary words they moved side by side towards the horses that Alita had brought out.

"I presume you know who I am?" Clint Wilbur asked after they had ridden a little way in silence.

"I suspect," Alita replied, "that you are the new owner of Marshfield House."

"Clint Wilbur—at your service!" he replied. "And you?"

"My name is Alita ... Blair."

"You work for the Duke?"

"Yes, I train his horses."

"He told me that he had some he would like to sell."

"I think you will find that our horses are outstanding," Alita said.

"And they are all for sale!"

There was a dry note in his voice which made her laugh.

"Have you had a great number offered to you already?"

"Enough to fill the *Mayflower* a thousand times over!"

She laughed again.

"Well, before you make any decision, have a look at the Langstone Stables. I promise you it will be worthwhile."

"I am prepared to take your word for that. You are an exceptional rider, Miss Blair."

"Thank you," she said. "And though it may sound very forward, I would like to return the compliment."

There was no doubt, she thought, that he was a rider whom it would be a privilege to provide with a proper mount.

There was something easy about the way he sat a horse, as if he belonged to it, and she was sure that like herself he felt happier and more at home in the saddle than anywhere else.

"Well?" he said after a moment. "Why do you not ask the question that is in your mind?"

She looked at him in surprise.

"What do you imagine that is?"

"You are wondering which part of America I come from, so let me tell you, it is Texas."

"Of course!" she exclaimed. "I might have guessed it! I have always been told that they have better riders, and finer horses, in Texas than anywhere else."

"I see they have taught you something in England besides class distinctions and etiquette," he said.

"They taught us how to breed good horse-flesh!" Alita retorted. "And that is something you will, I know, appreciate."

They had reached the horses by now and the stable-boys who were holding them stared at Clint Wilbur in undisguised curiosity.

"This is Double Star," Alita said, dismounting with a swift movement, and patting the neck of the horse as she spoke, "but I would like you to go round the course first on King Hal. He is the best jumper of the three."

Clint Wilbur swung himself into the saddle and rode off.

Alita watched him go and knew by the way he was handling King Hal that the horse would show itself off to its best advantage.

The Race for Love

She watched him take every jump faultlessly, and when he came back to her there was a smile on his lips and she thought his eyes seemed even bluer than they had before.

"What do you think of him?" she asked.

"I want to try the others first," he answered, "before I waste all my adjectives on this one."

She laughed as he mounted Red Trump and rode away.

* * *

Driving in State to the Castle for dinner, Clint Wilbur thought that at least this evening would not be so formal or boring as he had found a large number of dinner-parties in England to be.

He and the Duke would certainly have an agreeable topic in common, and that was his horses.

They were indeed outstanding, and Clint Wilbur intended to buy them, but only at a sensible price. He congratulated himself on having been clever enough to try them out before spending the evening with their owner.

This last week he had been taken by a member of the Jockey Club to see his stud at Epsom.

He had made it quite clear to Clint Wilbur that he expected to sell his horses to him for sums that even the merest greenhorn would have known to be exorbitant.

Clint Wilbur had in fact been ready to dig in his toes and refuse to buy what was being pressed upon him long before he reached the stable at Epsom.

The horses actually proved to be a disappointment.

He would not have bought one of them in any circumstances, and he was well aware as they drove back to London that he had not only annoyed the man who had given him an expensive luncheon but had incurred an enemy.

This was the sort of experience which he found

distasteful. At the same time, he had learnt many years ago that he was a target for every crook, sharpster, and charlatan who wished to get their hands on his money.

He had bought Marshfield House not only because he liked it and knew the hunting in this part of England was exceptionally good, but also because it was a bargain.

Compared to the other Estates he had been offered, he thought, he was getting his money's worth, and it gave him a sense of satisfaction to know that in that instance at any rate he had not been outsmarted.

Money had been so much a part of Clint Wilbur's life ever since he was old enough to know it was there that he accepted it casually, but with certain reservations.

He knew it gave him power, and also that because he was so rich he often saw people in a different light from what they actually were.

"When a person is as rich as you are," someone had once said to him, "he views life through a glass window, which keeps him from coming into contact with reality. People talk to you in a different voice, and with a different expression on their faces, from the one they would use with ordinary folk."

That was true, Clint Wilbur had found, and as he grew older he realised how two-faced people could be where he was concerned. It had not made him cynical or bitter, but merely cautious and perhaps at times over-suspicious.

He thought when he received the Duke's most effusive invitation to dine at Langstone Castle the night he arrived in the County that he had either a marriageable daughter or something to sell.

It had not taken him long to discover that the Duke's horses were a very saleable property, and he was wondering as he was shown into the large and impressive Drawing-Room whether a marriageable daughter would materialise.

When he saw Hermione and heard the proud note in the Duke's voice when he presented her, he knew exactly what was implied.

Chapter Two

Clint Wilbur arrived at the race-course to find, as he had anticipated, that Alita was already there.

She was riding a different horse from those he had seen before, a grey that he thought seemed almost too small and elegant for the high jumps.

But the grey took them in style, and as Alita drew level with him he saw that she was smiling under the tattered jockey-cap she wore as usual.

"You are early!" she said accusingly.

"You did not expect me?"

"I thought you would come later, since you were out last night."

Even as she spoke she thought perhaps it was a mistake to admit that she knew he had dined at the Castle. After all, it was not usual for those in the stables to know what went on in the Reception-Rooms.

Clint Wilbur did not appear to think it strange. He merely said:

"I thought I would have another look at the horses before I inspect them officially this morning in the Duke's presence."

"He is bringing you to the stables?" Alita asked.

"At eleven-thirty A.M.," Clint Wilbur answered.

"I want to be sure of my ground before I start bargaining."

"Is that what you intend to do?"

"People seldom ask for the sum they expect finally to receive," he replied.

Alita thought that her uncle would be disappointed, but she was silent and after a moment Clint Wilbur went on:

"I admire the horse you are riding."

He saw a sudden expression of alarm in her eyes. Then she said quietly:

"Flamingo is not for sale."

He sensed that there was a reason for the sharpness of her voice, and he asked:

"Why not? I understood from the Duke that every horse in the stables was at my disposal."

"Flamingo belongs to me."

Clint Wilbur raised his eye-brows and said:

"If you keep him in the Duke's stables, I suppose I shall see him this morning when I inspect the other horses."

"Not if I can help it!"

Alita was talking in an abrupt manner which told him that she was disturbed.

But he was curious, and because he wished to probe deeper he said:

"You are making me suspicious. Am I being palmed off with inferior goods while someone else is having the pick of the bunch?"

"No, no! It is nothing like that," Alita said. "But Flamingo is mine. I have had him ever since he was a foal, and he is different from all the other horses."

"In what way?"

She looked at him searchingly and his blue eyes met hers with a query in them.

After a moment she said:

"If I show you what Flamingo can do, will you try to ... understand?"

"I will certainly try."

Alita hesitated, as if she were still undecided as to whether he was trustworthy or not. Then she said, almost as if she spoke to herself:

"I have to ... convince you."

As she spoke she bent forward to pat Flamingo's neck and then gave him an order.

Clint Wilbur understood that she did not wish him to move, and he kept his horse at a standstill as she rode round in a circle in front of him.

Flamingo moved at an even pace, then at the word of command he trotted and reared up on his hind legs, walked for a few paces, then trotted again and repeated the performance.

When he had completed the circle, Alita, humming softly, made him waltz. Round and round he went, keeping in time to the music of her voice.

Afterwards he reversed before she took him into the centre of the circle, and once again he reared up on his hind legs, pawing the air with his front ones.

Then, going down on one knee with his other foreleg stuck out in front of him, he bowed his head three times to Clint Wilbur.

When the performance was over, Alita looked at the American for the first time and rode Flamingo to his side.

"Magnificent!" he said.

"There are other tricks he can do," Alita said, "but those are the ones at which he is faultless, however many times he repeats them."

"Flamingo has a very experienced teacher."

"I started when he was only a few months old," Alita explained. "He will of course follow me everywhere and come when I call him even if he is several fields away. He will leap a five-bar gate to obey me."

"I am very impressed!" Clint Wilbur said.

"I cannot part with him. He is all I have ... the only one ... in the world who ... loves me."

There was an unmistakable throb in her voice, and after a moment, as Clint Wilbur did not speak, she said:

"Please ... do not ask to see him when you come to the Castle this morning. I only brought him here today because he needed the exercise, and I thought you would not arrive until later."

It was in fact only just after six o'clock, and the trunks of the trees in the woods were still enveloped with the morning mist.

"I did not mention last night to His Grace the fact that I had already seen some of the horses," Clint Wilbur said.

"I am glad about that."

"I had the feeling that you would not wish me to do so," he went on, "and also I felt rather embarrassed in case His Grace should resent that I was trespassing on his property."

"And I do not think ... the Duke would approve of my showing you his horses," Alita said.

She was in fact quite sure that her uncle and aunt would be furious if they thought she was meeting any man surreptitiously, and especially Clint Wilbur!

She was surprised, however, that he was perceptive enough to realise that she would not wish the Duke to know that he had already seen and ridden several of his horses.

She had in fact been apprehensive all the evening in case she should get into trouble for not reporting what had happened.

As if he knew she was relieved by his discretion, Clint Wilbur said:

"It is very easy to make mistakes in England, where there is so much protocol. As my countrymen say, one has only to open one's mouth to put one's foot in it!"

Alita laughed, as he had meant her to do.

"I think, however," he said, "that because I have

had a very Cosmopolitan education, you can trust me to be tactful."

"You have been to Europe before?"

"Many times," he answered, "but only for occasional and very short visits to England. That is why I am rather intrigued to be an English land-owner."

"Marshfield House is magnificent!"

"You know it well?" he asked.

"I have been to the stables since its owner died," she answered. "They are not as light and airy as ours, but if you would spend money on them there are a great many improvements which would be well worth making."

"I see I shall have to ask you to advise me."

She glanced at him quickly and he thought that she imagined he was being sarcastic.

"That is an invitation," he said. "I can see that you are very knowledgeable about horses, and the way they need to be housed in this country is different from the way they are allowed to run almost wild in Texas."

"I would love to know how they are trained there," Alita said. "I have read everything I can about the methods used in different countries, but most books, even if I can get hold of them are seldom very informative."

"I will see if I can find you one," Clint Wilbur said. "Do you read a lot?"

"All the time," Alita said. "It is the only way I can..."

She stopped suddenly.

She had been about to say: "keep in touch with the world outside the Castle," but she knew it would be indiscreet.

She thought that he was about to question what she had been going to say, and so she was glad that at that moment they joined the other horses waiting with the stable-boys.

"I would like to race you," Clint Wilbur said.

"May I choose my own mount so that you do not steal a march on me?"

"I have a feeling that you are accusing me of being unsporting," Alita replied; "but of course the choice is yours."

She liked the way he inspected each horse, looking for the good points that she knew so well, and she was certain that he missed none of the flaws.

Finally he said:

"I will ride Rajah."

The stable-boy, on Alita's instructions, transferred the saddle from his own horse.

"What is your choice?" Clint Wilbur asked. "And may I say that I still think I am somewhat handicapped."

"I doubt it," she said. "And I think it would be appropriate if I rode Wild West. He is one of the youngest horses in the stables, but one for which I have great hopes."

Wild West already carried a side-saddle, and Alita tightened the girth a little before, without any help, she sprang into the saddle with a lightness which made it appear almost as if she flew through the air.

"Twice round the course," she said, "is about the same distance as the Cheltenham Hunt Plate."

"Twice around it shall be!" Clint Wilbur said. "How shall we start?"

She felt that he was deliberately and with a slight air of condescension letting her arrange the race, as if he was sure that because he was a man he would beat her but was prepared to give her a "chance."

She pulled her jockey-cap a little farther down over her forehead, and turning to the stable-boys she said:

"Ned, count slowly up to three, then say: 'Go!' Do you understand?"

"Aye, Miss Alita. Oi understands."

"Very well," Alita said. "Start now, and count slowly."

The boy counted aloud:

"One—two—three ... Go!"

Alita moved off a little faster than did Clint Wilbur, and she was just ahead of him as they reached the first jump.

Wild West took it superbly, with a foot to spare, and Rajah, guided by the American's skilful hands, spread himself out faultlessly.

Then they started down the ride at a speed that made Alita feel as if the crisp air almost cut her cheeks.

She was determined to win and she knew too that she had an advantage in that she was lighter than the American, but she had to admit that he rode superbly.

The horses were more or less evenly matched except that Wild West would have run himself out at the very beginning of the race had not Alita been able to keep him under control.

He almost pulled her arms out of their sockets before she finally made him settle down.

After they had gone round the course once she knew exactly the place where she would give Wild West his head, and finish, she hoped, in front of Clint Wilbur.

But she saw as she took the last fence that he was half a length ahead of her and she acknowledged that it was his superb horsemanship that made Rajah move faster than he had ever moved before.

Wild West, with Alita's urging, made a sudden sprint at the very last moment, but Clint Wilbur was undoubtedly a neck ahead as they passed the cheering stable-boys.

Riding into the centre of the course, they drew their horses slowly to a standstill.

"You won!" Alita said breathlessly when finally she could speak.

"It was one of the best races I have ever ridden!" Clint Wilbur said. "Thank you, Miss Blair. I have not enjoyed anything so much for many years!"

"It was exciting!" Alita agreed. "I have never ridden a genuine race on this course before, although sometimes Sam and I ride the horses together to get them used to having competition."

"Who is Sam?" he enquired.

"His Grace's Head-Groom. You will meet him this morning. He is wonderful with horses."

"As you are."

"I am so lucky to have them."

"Then what will happen if I take them all away from you?"

"We will still have the mares and quite a number of foals," Alita replied.

She explained how the late Duke had spent a great deal of money in breeding thoroughbreds and how she hoped that some of the money for the horses which were sold would go into buying new stock.

"Will you mind losing those you have trained so well?" Clint Wilbur asked.

"It is always like losing a very close friend," Alita said simply, "but I will still have ... Flamingo."

She glanced at him as she spoke, and he thought she was still apprehensive that he might demand Flamingo with the others.

"If you say he is your horse," Clint Wilbur said after a moment, "how could the Duke sell him without your permission?"

Alita drew in a deep breath as she quickly tried to think of an answer.

"His Grace has been kind enough," she said at length, "to let me keep Flamingo in his stables; but I think if it was a question of a good offer from a valued client, he would not expect me to refuse to sell."

It sounded rather a weak explanation, but she thought Clint Wilbur accepted it.

He said nothing, and when he had dismounted he remarked:

"I intend to go home now. There are certain people I have to see before I come to the Castle to meet the Duke."

The stable-boys were transferring the saddle from Rajah's back onto his own horse, and Alita, lowering her voice so that they could not hear what she said, pleaded:

"You will not forget that you have never seen me before?"

"I have a retentive memory," Clint Wilbur replied. "But as I hope to meet you here again and certainly to challenge you to another race, I can assure you that my lips are sealed."

"Thank you," she said with a smile.

Then, without waiting for him to leave, she mounted one of the waiting horses and rode off round the course.

* * *

When Alita arrived back at the Castle to change from her riding-habit into an ugly brown dress which came first to hand when she opened her wardrobe, she thought that the race she had run against Clint Wilbur was one of the most exciting things she had ever done.

She was so used to spending most of her days working in the stables and talking only to Sam that the mere fact that she could discuss horses with anyone as knowledgeable as Clint Wilbur was something she had never expected to happen to her.

She had often longed not to meet the usual guests who came to the Castle—her isolation from them did not trouble her at all—but to talk to the Duke's more intelligent visitors and especially to those who came from overseas.

The books she had read—and fortunately the Library was a very comprehensive one, if slightly out-of-date—made her feel that in her imagination she had travelled to many places.

She knew the habits and customs of peoples whom she was well aware she would never in her life have the chance of seeing or meeting.

America had fascinated her because the recent development of so large a Continent was such a contrast to the traditions of the Old World.

She liked the idea of a country where men thought they were not only free but equal, and she thought that the easy manner in which Clint Wilbur spoke to her was very different from the way which would have been adopted by any of Hermione's admirers.

Thinking her to be nothing but a stable-girl, they would of course be polite, but undoubtedly condescending, talking down to her and certainly not on equal terms.

"Mr. Wilbur is charming," Alita told herself, "and also intelligent. Hermione will be lucky if he marries her."

She could not help thinking with a touch of amusement that if there was any condescending to be done, it would be on Hermione's part.

The Duchess had made it quite clear that she did not think that the Americans were on a Social par with the English Aristocracy.

But money would undoubtedly cover a great number of deficiencies in a family-tree and Alita knew that the Duke would welcome Clint Wilbur as a son-in-law with open arms.

It seemed absurd that, living in a huge Castle, owning thousands of acres of land, and having a Social position that was unequalled, the Duke should find it extremely hard to make ends meet.

But it was the truth, and only Alita knew of the cheese-paring that went on in the Castle, the low wages the servants were paid, and the continual nagging over the housekeeping bills.

Even Hermione had to go without a great number of things she desired, and her gowns were made over, refurbished and retrimmed a dozen times, before they were finally discarded in favour of Alita.

This was a doubtful pleasure because Hermione, although the same height as Alita, was considerably larger in build.

Alita was slim and the amount of exercise she took made it impossible for her to have an ounce of superfluous flesh on her body.

While naked she had the figure of a young goddess, and when she was dressed in Hermione's discarded clothes, which had been clumsily altered by the village seamstress, she looked lumpy and a mess.

What was more, because the Duchess was parsimonious and did not like her niece, she insisted before handing them over that Hermione's gowns should first have removed the trimmings and any decoration that might be used again.

The brown dress, for instance, which was so unbecoming and which had been chosen mistakenly in a bad light, had been trimmed with yards and yards of ecru lace, which had taken away the severity of the colour.

It had in fact when it first arrived at the Castle been quite an attractive gown.

Hermione, however, had never liked it, for she preferred dresses in bright pinks and blues, which did not suit Alita. She usually left them hanging in the wardrobe after the village seamstress had done her worst with them.

She had told herself until she grew to believe it that it was not of the slightest consequence what she wore, and the horses would not distinguish any difference in her appearance.

They loved her for the softness of her voice, for

the love which they knew she gave them, and for the certain magic which made her able to tame and train even the wildest of yearlings.

Absent-mindedly, with her thoughts still on the race, Alita stuck several more pins into the bun at the back of her head, leaving it no more tidy than it had been before, then went downstairs to the Breakfast-Room.

When there were people staying at the Castle or guests came to meals, she fetched a tray of food from the kitchen and either ate it in a small room which had once been used by a Housekeeper or took it up to her bed-room.

Often she did not even bother to do that.

She merely walked about the kitchen, helping herself to some food and assisting old Mrs. Henderson, who had been at the Castle for years and who was finding it exceedingly difficult to carry on with the inadequate village girls which were all the help the Duke could afford to give her.

Alita would eat scraps while she stirred sauces or tossed a salad, and Mrs. Henderson would chatter about the "old days" when her grandfather had been alive.

Then, there had been a whole army of servants to keep the Castle in the way it was meant to be kept.

"Thirty stayin' in t'house, if you'd believe it, Miss Alita!" Mrs. Henderson would say. "An' all the ladies bringin' their lady's-maids, and the gent'men with their valets and grooms an' horses an' all!"

"And parties every night, of course," Alita would prompt, having heard the story a hundred times before.

"I seldom had less than fifty to dinner, Miss, an' a Ball on a Sat'day night with both dinner an' supper to prepare for."

"It must have been hard work!"

"Not half as hard as it be these days!" Mrs. Henderson replied. "I'd three trained assistants, an' as many scullery-maids as I wanted, an' four in the Still-Room. Think of it, Miss, four! If you could on'y see the teas they provided when the gent'men came in from shootin' or huntin'."

"It makes me feel hungry just to think of it," Alita said with a smile.

"An' never less than a dozen courses for dinner," Mrs. Henderson continued as if Alita had not spoken. "The ladies in their tiaras, His Grace wearin' th' Order o' the Garter—those were the days!"

At this point Mrs. Henderson would usually break off to scold one of the kitchen-maids for ceasing to turn the spit or for burning a piece of toast.

"I can't take me eyes off anyone in this kitchen, an' that's a fact!" she would say disgustedly.

Alita would find it equally fascinating to sit in the pantry and hear from Barnes, the old Butler, who had been a footman in her grandfather's time, what the table had looked like with the Langstone silver decorating it and the great Gold Cup displayed in the centre.

That had now been sold, as had a lot of other treasures. In fact, Alita knew that items of value left the Castle every year.

It was like an Aladdin's cave, she thought, depleted by thieves until finally there would be nothing left.

She could understand that her uncle was struggling to keep the place in some sort of order for his son Gerald, but unless the Marquis could return from India as rich as a Nabob, there was only Hermione left to save the situation.

Certainly the solution would be for Hermione to marry Clint Wilbur, and Alita as she entered the Breakfast-Room was exceedingly curious to hear what Hermione had thought of their guest of the night before.

But the only person seated at the table was the Duchess.

"You are late again, Alita!" she exclaimed, without preliminary greeting, as her niece entered.

"I am sorry, Aunt Emily, but I was with the horses, and I knew you would want me to change before I came to breakfast."

"Naturally," the Duchess replied. "I will not have you sitting down in riding-boots. We must observe some decency."

"That is why I am late, Aunt Emily, and I apologise," Alita said.

She sat down at the table and helped herself from the first dish that was offered to her.

Hermione then came into the room.

She was looking extremely pretty and elegant in a gown of sky-blue trimmed profusely with broderie anglaise.

"Good-morning, my dearest," the Duchess said in a very different tone from the one she had always used towards her niece.

"Good-morning, Mama. Good-morning, Alita!" Hermione said. "Where is Papa?"

"I am here!" the Duke replied from the door. "And there is something which will interest you and your mother in the post."

"What is it, Lionel?" the Duchess asked.

"An invitation to Windsor Castle!"

Hermione gave a little shriek.

"Oh, Papa!"

"Her Majesty is giving a family-party and Ball for the bridle-couple, and I must say I am extremely gratified that we should be among the guests."

Princess Beatrice, the Queen's favourite daughter, had been married to Prince Henry of Battenberg at the end of July, and this was to be an intimate party to which only relatives and those who enjoyed the Queen's friendship would be invited.

"It is a great honour, Lionel," the Duchess said, "and a delightful opportunity for Hermione to make new friends."

"I have always wanted to stay at Windsor Castle!" Hermione said. "But I shall need some new gowns."

"Yes, of course," the Duchess said; "your father cannot expect you to appear at such an occasion looking like Cinderella!"

"Well, how much you can spend depends entirely on Alita," the Duke remarked.

"On Alita?" the Duchess questioned incredulously.

"Clint Wilbur is coming over this morning to decide which of our horses he will purchase."

"And you intend to have Alita there?"

"I consider it essential that she be present," the Duke replied.

He saw that the Duchess was about to argue, and he said:

"Alita knows more about the horses than anyone else. If you expect to have money to spend on Hermione's new gowns, Alita will certainly get more than Bates, who is past it, or from Sam, who does not understand money."

"Then I suppose I must permit her to meet Mr. Wilbur," the Duchess said; "but not, of course, as your niece."

"No, no, of course not!" the Duke answered, then coughed to remind his wife that the servants were in the room.

"What did you think of our American neighbour?" the Duke asked Hermione in an over-hearty voice to cover up his wife's indiscretion.

"I thought he was very pleasant," Hermione said, "but rather difficult to talk to."

"Really?" the Duke answered. "I found him very easy."

"He did not pay me compliments," Hermione said, as she began to pout.

"I would have thought it extremely pushing of him if he had done so," the Duchess interposed. "The Latin peoples may behave in that way, but one does not expect it from English-speaking gentlemen."

"No, of course not," the Duke agreed before Hermione could speak. "At the same time, he is eligible, very eligible, and I have often thought that the two Estates would merge very comfortably together."

Alita thought that what the Duke really meant was that if Clint Wilbur were his son-in-law, he could be persuaded to defray most of the expenses incurred on the Langstone property.

However, Alita said nothing but merely went on eating her breakfast, until at last when the Duke and Duchess had left the room she and Hermione were alone together.

"I am longing to hear what you thought of Mr. Wilbur," Alita said in a tone to which Hermione invariably responded.

"Do not tell Papa and Mama," she replied, "but I was rather disappointed in him."

"You were?"

"He is good-looking in a way," Hermione continued, "but very sure of himself, which I did not expect from an American, and I had a feeling that he was not as bowled over by me as I thought he would be."

"I am sure you are mistaken," Alita said.

"You did not hear him."

Hermione gave a little sigh as she said:

"Oh, Alita, if only William Swindley had Mr. Wilbur's money!"

"Are you in love with Lord Swindley?"

"I dare not let myself be," Hermione answered. "You know he has not a penny in the world, and his crumbling old Manor-House in Surrey is even more dilapidated than the Castle."

"And he loves you?"

"He says he does, and he proposes to me every time I see him. He also writes to me almost every day."

Alita looked at her cousin wide-eyed.

"How have you managed to keep Aunt Emily from knowing about that?"

Hermione smiled.

"Barnes sorts the letters."

Alita laughed. She knew that old Barnes had adored Hermione ever since she was born.

He had always kept the largest peaches for her and the ripest grapes!

She remembered staying at the Castle when she was a child and being jealous because Barnes would even hide several of the sugared comfits which were put on the table at dinner-parties, to give to Hermione the next morning.

"Would Uncle Lionel mind if you married Lord Swindley?" she asked.

"He has set his heart on my having a rich husband," Hermione answered, "and I must say I agree with him, Alita. I could not bear to go on fussing over every penny as we have to do now."

She gave a little sigh and continued:

"If I have to hear Mama complaining that we are hard-up for very much longer I think I shall scream!"

Alita felt much the same and she sympathised with Hermione. But she wondered if she would be happy with Clint Wilbur when she certainly could not share his obsession for horses.

Hermione rose from the table and crossed the room to stand looking at herself in a gilt-framed mirror that hung on the wall.

It had been carved in the reign of Charles II

and there were the inevitable cupids holding up the crown and a number of hearts and love-knots also decorating the frame.

"Have you ever really been in love, Hermione?" Alita asked from behind her.

"I have begun once or twice to think I was," Hermione answered, "but I have always discovered that the men in question were poor, and that has put me off immediately!"

"I think if one was really in love one would not mind."

"I would mind," Hermione said firmly.

She went on staring into the mirror. Then she said:

"What is wrong with me that I do not attract rich men? There was a man in London this summer— Lord Sudbridge.

"Papa pushed us together in a way that was almost embarrassing, until finally he told me that he was secretly engaged to a girl he had loved for years. Papa was furious!"

"I think, Hermione, that you ought to consider your own happiness rather than what Uncle Lionel wants," Alita said. "He does not have to marry the man he chooses for you."

"I shall be happy if I am rich," Hermione replied. "I could have all the gowns I wanted and lots of jewellery and be able to go to parties night after night in London."

She paused, then said:

"On second thoughts, I think Mr. Wilbur will do me very well. He may be American, but then the Americans have far more money than anyone in this country."

"He comes from Texas," Alita said.

"How do you know that?" Hermione asked.

Alita realised that she had made a slip, and she answered:

"I suppose Uncle Lionel told me. Anyway, I know he does, and Texas is wild and not what you would call very civilised."

"If he is rich enough, I can stay in his house in New York when he goes to Texas, or anywhere else he has one," Hermione said in a practical tone. "It would not be difficult. All you have to do, Alita, is to get as much money out of him as you can."

"You cannot have it all," Alita said. "I want some of it."

"You?" Hermione said in surprise.

"I mean for the new blood-stock," Alita replied.

"Oh, that," Hermione replied. "Mama will be furious if you twist too much out of Papa."

"Uncle Lionel realises that what he invests in the horses pays a good dividend, and that is exactly what he is expecting now."

She felt that Hermione did not understand, so Alita added:

"Translated into practical language, that means gowns for you and more money to spend on entertaining."

"Then you must certainly have your share of the spoils, Alita," Hermione said, laughing. "But for goodness' sake, tidy yourself up before you see Mr. Wilbur, or your appearance will certainly lower the price."

Alita looked at her in surprise.

"Do you really think so?"

"Of course I do!" Hermione replied. "When people look rich and prosperous, one is always prepared to pay more."

"I never thought of that," Alita remarked.

"On the same principle," Hermione said, "one gives a better Christmas-present to one's rich friends than to one's poor."

"What a funny idea," Alita said. "I should have given the best present to the person I liked most."

"That is a very naïve way of looking at things,"

Hermione said. "If you had been in London with me this Season you would have seen that people went out of their way to do things for me, not because they liked me but because I am the daughter of a Duke."

"It sounds cynical for you to think like that."

"It is not a question of thinking, it is knowing. I even heard one girl say: 'We must ask Lady Hermione to the *best* party. After all, her father is a Duke.'"

Alita laughed.

"You are destroying my faith in human nature, not that I have much!"

As she spoke, she thought to herself that she had every reason to have no faith. She knew only too well that the friendships she had known in the past had not survived adversity, or rather a scandal.

Aloud she said:

"I must change and get back to the horses. Whatever I look like, they must look their best to impress Mr. Wilbur."

"Try and smarten yourself up," Hermione advised, "then whatever he offers you can look down your nose as if it was much too small a sum even to be considered."

"You—not I—ought to be selling the horses!" Alita laughed.

"I would very likely do it better," Hermione said, "except, as you well know, I know nothing about the beasts and have no wish to learn."

Alita thought again, as she left the room, that Clint Wilbur would not want a wife who did not share his interest in horses.

Then she told herself that she had always heard that opposites got on well together, and besides, no man really liked competition.

She wondered whether he would have minded if she had beaten him on the race-course that morning.

Perhaps his masculine dignity would have been affronted. In consequence he might not have been as keen on buying the horses as she was quite certain he would be.

'It was wrong of me to try to beat Clint Wilbur,' she thought to herself.

Yet, the challenge had been irresistible.

She could feel again the excitement of striving with every nerve in her body to defeat him, but he had won and she had known by the expression on his face that he was delighted to have done so.

She went upstairs to her bed-room to change into her habit, and because of what Hermione had said to her she realised perhaps for the first time how very worn and threadbare it was.

There was nothing she could do about it but she did try to find a shirt that had not lost a button at the neck and she did look through her drawers to find if she had stockings such as she wore out hunting.

She found to her dismay that the only two she possessed were frayed at the edges and also were dirty.

She had meant to wash and press them but there never seemed to be time, and there was certainly no-one in the Castle who would wait on her.

"He will just have to take me as I am," she told herself sharply.

Then she took down from the shelf in the wardrobe her hunting top-hat.

She put it on her head, then realised how untidy her hair was, and searching through her drawer she found a chignon, which she also wore out hunting.

She put it over her bun, placed the hat on top of her head, and thought she looked a little tidier although she was certain, whatever Hermione might say, that Clint Wilbur would notice no difference in her.

At least, she thought, she had made the effort, whether or not it would make the slightest difference to the price Mr. Wilbur was prepared to pay for the horses.

She hoped not, as she put on her riding-boots and realised that they had not been cleaned for weeks.

It was hard enough to get her uncle's boots polished in the manner he expected, but though Alita occasionally cleaned her boots herself when she was going hunting, she again realised that there was no-one who would notice what she wore.

There were two packs of hounds in the County, of which the Quexby was extremely fashionable and the membership was very expensive.

The Hunting-Lodges which belonged to the important and rich sportsmen would be filled during the winter with members of the aristocracy.

Hermione of course hunted with the Quexby and Alita often longed to do so herself, but she knew that it was a thrill which she was never likely to experience.

The other pack, which she was permitted to join, belonged to the farmers who could not afford to pay the fees of a fashionable hunt and who therefore felt out-of-place amongst the gentry.

They had come to an amicable arrangement over which part of the County the different packs hunted, and naturally the Quexby took the best of everything. Only that which they did not want was left for the farmers.

It was enough as far as Alita was concerned, and they were all very pleasant to her, although she was aware that she did not fit in amongst them.

All that really concerned her was to try out the horses she was training, to be in the front of the field and in at the kill.

This she always managed to achieve, and she

would in fact have been surprised if she had heard the compliments on her horsemanship that were paid her behind her back.

She was thinking, as she went towards the stables, that if Clint Wilbur bought the majority of her uncle's horses and there were few left for her to hunt with, she would at least still have Flamingo.

It was more important to her than anything else that she and Flamingo, whom she loved and who loved her, should not be separated.

She reached the stables and found that Sam too had smartened himself up, having polished the silver buttons of his waist coat and also his boots.

What was much more important was that the stables themselves were exceedingly spick-and-span.

A neatly plaited piece of straw had been placed in front of the door of each stall, every horse had been freshly bedded down, and even the yard had been freshly watered and brushed.

"Keep your fingers crossed, Sam," Alita said.

As she finished making sure that everything was as she wanted it to be, she heard the sound of her uncle's voice coming from the direction of the house.

"It's up to you, Miss Alita," Sam said.

They both waited, looking not at the Duke but at the tall, handsome man with blue eyes walking beside him.

Chapter Three

Clint Wilbur's inspection of the horses in the stables was finished and the Duke looked at him with an unmistakable expression of greed.

He had been so overwhelmingly effusive about his horses that Alita felt embarrassed.

She could understand only too well her uncle's need of money. At the same time, some pride within her made her feel that it was undignified of the Duke of Langstone to play so unashamedly the part of a supplicant.

'It is very bad for a young man to have so much power,' she thought.

In consequence, she could not help, although she knew it would annoy her uncle, speaking in a colder voice about the horses than she would have done under other circumstances.

She even pointed out two or three faults, which brought a frown to the Duke's forehead, but she was certain that with his expert knowledge Clint Wilbur had already noticed them.

They finished by looking at two or three of the younger horses which were not yet fully trained.

"You would not be able to hunt with them this year," Alita said, "but they will undoubtedly be in excellent form by next autumn."

Barbara Cartland

"Of course, I might not be here another year," Clint Wilbur replied.

Alita thought that he was only pretending a reluctance because there was going on between them a duel of words that was somehow stimulating.

If he was disparaging, she found an answer, and if he sounded effusive, she cooled him down.

It was for Alita a thrilling experience to spar with a man and to know that as they did so they were both using personal experience and exceptional knowledge of horsemanship in a way that the Duke would not understand.

Nevertheless, she waited to hear what Clint Wilbur had to say, knowing that he was impressed despite the fact that his face was expressionless.

"I congratulate Your Grace!" he said to the Duke. "I have seldom seen so many horses in such outstanding condition, and for that I suppose I should commend Miss Blair."

"She certainly works very hard," the Duke answered, "but I was fortunate to inherit from my father blood-stock that is almost unequalled in this country."

"You also inherited some exceptionally well-built stables," Clint Wilbur said.

"They certainly had enough money spent on them," the Duke replied drily.

"I noticed you have a race-course near our boundary," Clint Wilbur remarked.

"That also was laid out by my father," the Duke answered, "and I hope you will avail yourself of it. I believe Miss Blair has had the fences repaired."

"Thank you!" Clint Wilbur smiled. "I feel sure that these horses, if they are transferred to Marshfield, would miss the jumps."

The Duke waited, with a glint in his eye.

"What I am going to suggest," Clint Wilbur said

slowly, "is that I purchase a great number, perhaps all, of your horses—on one condition."

"Condition?" the Duke queried.

"It is that you assist me to provide them with the accommodation to which they are accustomed."

The Duke looked surprised, and Clint Wilbur went on:

"I imagine that the person who will know best what they want and what is unsatisfactory with the stables at Marshfield House is Miss Blair."

Alita turned to stare at him with startled eyes.

She remembered that he had given her an invitation to visit his stables and tell him what was wrong, but she had not thought he meant it seriously.

"What are you suggesting?" the Duke asked.

"I am asking you to lend me Miss Blair to show me how the stables can be improved and what alterations should be made before the horses are moved there."

The Duke was astonished, and Alita was aware that he was thinking that it would be extremely unconventional and would certainly earn her aunt's disapproval if she went to Marshfield House unchaperoned.

"I already have a great many workmen in the house," Clint Wilbur went on, "and an architect who has a big reputation in London, but I am quite certain he knows nothing about housing horses."

"I do not think I can spare Miss Blair," the Duke said at length.

"I quite understand," Clint Wilbur replied. "In which case, I shall be sorry to lose your horses, but I daresay I can manage with those I have already."

As he spoke, he walked out the stable-door to stand in the yard.

Alita gave the Duke a frantic glance, and he hurried after the American. As he joined him he said:

"Surely, Wilbur, you cannot mean that your purchase of my horses is entirely dependent upon having Miss Blair's advice?"

"I am afraid so," Clint Wilbur replied casually. "I would not like to take these horses from their excellent accommodation and place them in stables which I know to be unsatisfactory."

Alita knew that the Duke was turning the problem over in his mind. Then his desire for money overcame every other consideration.

"Of course, if it means so much to you, my dear fellow," he said, "I am sure Miss Blair will do anything you require."

"Thank you," Clint Wilbur said quietly.

There was an unmistakable look of satisfaction and amusement on his face as he turned to Alita.

"His Grace has very kindly asked me to luncheon," he said, "but I will send my groom back with my Chaise and tell him to have one of my horses here at two-thirty."

With difficulty Alita found her voice.

"P-perhaps ... you would care to ... ride one of ours?" she suggested. "I can ... easily lead it back when we have finished our ... b-business together."

There was a faint smile on Clint Wilbur's firm mouth as he replied:

"A good idea, Miss Blair! And I leave you to choose which horse you think will suit me best."

He walked away with the Duke, and Alita gave a sigh that seemed to come from the very depths of her being.

"I believe he meant what he said, Sam," she remarked to the old groom when the two gentlemen were out of earshot.

"Oi'm sure 'e did, Miss," replied Sam who had listened to the whole conversation. "An' if ye asks me, 'e's a gen'leman as knows 'is own mind."

"He certainly does that!" Alita said. "And I have a feeling, Sam, that we are going to have a tough time bargaining with him."

"Oi'll leaves that to ye, Miss Alita," Sam replied with a grin; "ye be a darn' sight better at it than Oi am!"

* * *

The Duke's horse was waiting for Clint Wilbur when after an excellent luncheon he walked down the steps.

"Miss Blair will join you when you are away from the Castle," the Duke said in a low voice.

He had in fact sent an urgent message to Alita to be waiting for Mr. Wilbur in one of the fields that led towards Marshfield House.

She had anticipated that that was the best course anyway, being quite certain that the Duke would wish to keep from the Duchess any knowledge of what was happening.

When Alita went back to the Castle before luncheon she had gone into her cousin's room to find Hermione in a flutter over which gown she should wear.

"I want to look my best, Alita," she said, "and I cannot make up my mind whether the blue gown with the velvet ribbons suits me best, or the pink with the big bow on the bustle."

Alita considered the question seriously before she replied:

"I like you best in the blue, because it matches your eyes."

"Very well, I will wear the blue," Hermione said to her lady's-maid. "And hurry up! I want to make an entrance as soon as Papa takes Mr. Wilbur into the Drawing-Room."

She would certainly do that, Alita thought, for Hermione was looking exceedingly pretty, with her fair hair waved onto the top of her head, and the small fringe which had become the universal vogue amongst the fashionable young ladies.

In the light of the sun coming in through the

window, Hermione's skin was flawless, and the perfectly fitting blue gown accentuated the curves of her breasts while the tight corset she wore reduced the size of her waist.

"You have laced me so tight," Hermione complained to her maid, "that I can hardly breathe."

"Never mind," Alita said with a smile, "you look very elegant and very lovely!"

She thought that Clint Wilbur would be blind if he did not think so, and, being an American, he was certain to be impressed with the fact that Hermione was the daughter of a Duke!

Besides, what could be a more grand and romantic background than the Castle?

'In fact, everything an American millionaire could want!' she thought as she went back to her own bed-room.

When she reached it she looked in the mirror with a little grimace of amusement.

Despite her efforts to try to look smarter and more prosperous, as Hermione had advised, the exertion of inspecting the horses had brought the usual wisps of hair falling round her cheeks.

Her top-hat had slipped to an angle and the white shirt which she had buttoned tightly round her neck had once again burst a button.

"What does it matter?" Alita asked herself. "He was not looking at me. I am sure that he made up his mind to buy the horses when he took King Hal and Rajah over the jumps."

At the same time, she had the uncomfortable feeling that if her uncle had not acceded to Mr. Wilbur's request that she should advise him concerning the stables at Marshfield House, he would have stuck to his decision and left the horses where they were.

There was a steel-like quality about Clint Wilbur which she had never found in any other man.

The Race for Love

'I expect I will be able to tell him what is wrong with his stables this afternoon,' Alita thought to herself. 'Then, once the horses are at Marshfield House, I shall never see him again.'

She wondered why the thought was so depressing.

Then she remembered that at Marshfield there was no race-course, and she was certain that Mr. Wilbur would want to use theirs.

Because she expected that nobody would trouble about her luncheon, because there was a guest, Alita went down to the kitchen.

She helped herself to the dishes which came out of the Dining-Room, talking to Mrs. Henderson while she did so and assisting her by whipping up the cream for the apple-tart.

"I'm a-giving the gent'man proper English fare, seein' as he's American an' all," Mrs. Henderson said. "If he's going to live over here, he'll have to learn to enjoy what we eat."

"I suppose there is not much difference between our food and the sort they have in America," Alita replied, "except that we eat turkey only at Christmas-time, while they have it at other times of the year as well."

"That's all right for a big family," Mrs. Henderson said, "but His Grace'd soon get tired of turkey if I served it up to him often."

"I am sure he would," Alita replied. "He is looking forward to the pheasant-season."

As she spoke, she wondered if Clint Wilbur would enjoy cover-shooting.

The Estate of Marshfield House in its late-owner's day had provided excellent shooting. It had belonged to a rich man whom Alita remembered as being a friend of her father and mother when she was a child.

He had a very large family, and in a most unusual manner for an Englishman had divided his fortune equally amongst them.

This meant that the eldest son could not afford the upkeep of a house as big as Marshfield and it had therefore had to be sold.

The Duke, and, Alita gathered, most of their neighbours, had been horrified at his ignoring the custom of primogeniture, which was absolutely traditional amongst the great land-owners and those who had titles.

Certainly her grandfather, who had given her father, his second son, a mere pittance as an allowance during his lifetime and had left him little more at his death, would have been scandalised at such a revolutionary idea.

"Uncle Lionel will leave everything to Cousin Gerald," Alita told herself, "which means that if Hermione gets one hundred pounds or so a year on his death she will be very lucky."

The Duke was therefore right in looking for a rich husband for his only daughter, and Mr. Wilbur could certainly give Hermione everything she desired and a great deal more besides.

When the last course was being taken into the Dining-Room, Alita went upstairs to put on her riding-hat again and tuck every wisp of hair she could find into the chignon.

She realised that the elastic was loose and told herself that she should try to buy a new one.

However, it was difficult for her to buy anything, for the simple reason that she had no money.

Everything she required was, as far as her aunt was concerned, provided for her by Hermione's cast-offs, and if she asked for anything personal it invariably meant a long argument and usually also a lecture on ingratitude.

'I will manage without it,' Alita decided. 'Who will notice me anyway?'

THE RACE FOR LOVE

Picking up her whip, she left the Castle by a side-door and went to the stables.

"Which horse have you sent to the front for Mr. Wilbur?" she asked Sam.

"Oi thinks Sparkling Knight took 'is fancy, Miss," Sam answered, "an' the boys 'ave saddled Flamingo for ye."

"Thank you, Sam. You had better start praying that I will bring home the bacon!"

Sam chuckled at her use of the stable-boys' expression.

"Don' ye let 'is Grace hear ye a-talking like that, Miss Alita, or 'e'll be sayin' as we're a bad influence on ye!"

"He will say that only if I cannot persuade Mr. Wilbur to pay up," Alita answered; "and I can assure you, Sam, I will do my best."

"Oi'm sure ye will, Miss Alita." Sam smiled. "Then us can buy some new yearlings from th' local horse-fairs. Oi 'as me eye on one already which Oi think'll take your fancy."

"Oh, Sam, how exciting!" Alita exclaimed. "But I had better go now in case Mr. Wilbur leaves earlier than we expect him to."

She knew that once Sam started describing a horse it took a long time, and as she rode out of the yard towards the fields on the other side of it she knew it was going to be a hard tussle to make her uncle relinquish as much money as she and Sam wished to spend.

She was putting Flamingo through some of his tricks when she saw Sparkling Knight coming towards her.

Clint Wilbur was riding him with that easy grace that she knew must be born in a man and could never be taught.

He took off his hat when he was level with her and said:

55

"I might have guessed you would be busy exercising Flamingo, so I am not going to apologise for keeping you waiting."

"You are actually exceptionally punctual," Alita replied. "Did you enjoy your luncheon?"

"Everybody was extremely affable," he answered, "but the Duke informs me that I am to do my bargaining with you, which I consider most unfair."

"Unfair?" Alita enquired.

"You are aware better than their owner how much I want his horses."

"Do you really want them?"

"I would find it very hard to resist jumping King Hal again or racing Rajah."

"I am afraid they will cost you rather a lot," Alita said tentatively.

"We will talk about that later," he replied.

They rode for some way before Alita asked:

"Would you really have refused to buy His Grace's horses if he had not agreed to my helping you with your stables?"

"I think perhaps I was being rather unsporting in betting on a certainty," Clint Wilbur replied.

Alita laughed.

"Do you always get your own way?"

"Always!" he replied. "Which is one of the compensations for being so rich!"

She looked at him in surprise.

"Do you need any compensations?"

"Yes."

"Why?"

He seemed to consider the question for a moment. Then he said:

"I think a man who is born rich misses the struggle to survive and to reach the top, which to his contemporaries is a natural part of their development."

"I never thought of that!" Alita exclaimed. "But I think I understand. It is rather like sharpening your

THE RACE FOR LOVE

teeth on a rusk when you are a baby, and when you are older, praying frantically for what you need and wondering if your prayers will be answered."

She spoke as if she was working out for herself what he was thinking.

"Exactly!" he replied. "And that is why, not having had to fight for the big things in life, I fight for the trivialities in a manner which I admit to myself is sometimes over-dramatic."

Alita laughed.

"You are very honest."

"That at least costs nothing."

They rode for a few minutes in silence. Then he asked:

"Are you very poor?"

"I own nothing except Flamingo."

"Why?"

"My father and mother are ... dead."

"You were better off when they were alive?"

"Yes."

The words seemed to be dragged from her.

Then, because she had no wish to discusss herself any further, she deliberately touched Flamingo in a way which made him prance about so that she drew a little ahead of Clint Wilbur and it was impossible to speak intimately.

When he joined her again she had the strange feeling that he realised what she had done.

As if he respected her reticence, they talked of other things as they crossed the border between the two Estates and rode for a short while until they saw Marshfield House ahead of them.

It was an enormous, magnificent Georgian Mansion, built about 1750, with an architectural style which Alita had always admired.

At the same time, it was awe-inspiring to realise that it belonged to one man, and a bachelor at that!

Impulsively, without choosing her words, she said:

Barbara Cartland

"You will have to marry and have at least a dozen children!"

"Are you deciding my future, Miss Blair?" he enquired.

"Actually I was thinking of the house rather than you."

"Well, that is a change, at any rate!"

"Are you always being ... exhorted to marry?"

"It is one of the suggestions which is never very far from any woman's thoughts," he answered. "They find a bachelor provocative, and I have yet to meet one of your sex who is not eternally scheming as to how I can be forced up the aisle."

Alita laughed and he added:

"Let me tell you, Miss Blair, once and for all, that I am allergic to orange-blossoms, and I am extremely happy as I am."

Alita could not help thinking that this would be a blow for her uncle and Hermione, but aloud she said:

"Then the only thing I can suggest is that you turn half the house into an Orphanage and the other half can become a Convent!"

"I asked you here to advise me on the stables," Clint Wilbur said. "Unless you intend to house some of the horses in the Ball-Room and others in the Salon and the Library ..."

"Not the Library!" Alita interposed. "They might eat the books!"

"I forgot you were interested in reading," he said. "I am prepared to concede the Library especially if you wish to borrow the volumes it contains."

Alita's eyes sparkled for a moment, then she told herself that he did not really mean it. He was only being polite and the invitation was just part of the badinage they were enjoying with each other.

They went nearer to the house and as the stables came in sight she said:

The Race for Love

"Before we go any farther, perhaps you had better tell me exactly what you want me to do."

"Wait until you see the stables and judge for yourself," Clint Wilbur replied.

She thought it was strange that he should rely on her and not on himself, but when finally they reached the stables and dismounted she understood.

She had never looked closely at the stables at Marshfield House with the idea of using them.

She had ridden over two or three times with Sam when the house was empty to decide if any of the horses that were for sale were what they required for breeding.

They had in fact been very inferior to anything that was at the Castle, and during their visits Alita had concerned herself only with the animals and not with the conditions in which they were stabled.

Now she saw at a glance what was wrong.

The stables had been designed as an artistic adjunct of the house itself; the architect had concentrated on the exterior effect and could not have known anything about horses.

The stalls were too small and too dark, and although there was plenty of space, the idea had obviously been to provide stabling for an enormous number of animals without worrying as to whether they were comfortable or not.

Walking round, Alita forgot everything except that the horses she had cared for and loved were to live here in the future.

"Well?" Clint Wilbur asked after she had been silent for a long time.

"It is going to cost you a lot of money," she replied apprehensively, almost as if she were speaking to her uncle.

Then she remembered how rich Clint Wilbur was reputed to be.

Barbara Cartland

"I want you to tell Mr. Durrant what you recommend," he said.

She had been so intent on what she was doing that Alita had not realised they had been joined by a middle-aged man who looked, she thought, exactly how she would have expected an architect to look.

She shook hands with the newcomer and said:

"If you remove the partitions between the stalls and allow half as much again for each stall, they will be the right size."

Mr. Durrant made a note on the pad he carried.

"And the mangers are in the wrong place, and too low," Alita went on. "It would be far better to buy a different sort..."

She talked on for perhaps ten minutes while Mr. Durrant made notes and Clint Wilbur said nothing.

She wanted new windows at the back of the stables and those that were already there made larger. She suggested that water should be pumped in a different manner and the number of improvements mounted item by item.

Finally, when she had finished, she looked apologetically at Clint Wilbur.

"I am afraid it is... rather a lot," she said nervously.

"See that it is done as quickly as possible," Clint Wilbur remarked to Mr. Durrant in a tone of authority.

"Very good, Sir. Shall I take some men off the Orangery and see to this first?"

"You cannot double the number of your workmen?"

"I could," Mr. Durrant said a little tentatively, "but..."

"Then do so!" Clint Wilbur commanded.

He walked away and Alita moved beside him. After a moment she said:

The Race for Love

"I cannot help feeling that you are rather like Marlborough or the Duke of Wellington going into battle!"

"It is a battle to get these people to understand that I want everything done now, at once," he replied.

"The English do not work like that. They like to take things slowly and steadily."

"Then I have a surprise coming to them," he said. "When I want something, I want it yesterday!"

Alita laughed again. Then she asked:

"Shall we talk about the ... prices you are ... prepared to pay for our horses?"

"We can do that in the house," Clint Wilbur said. "There is something else I want to show you."

They entered the house by a side-door and she expected him to turn left, which would have led them to the centre of the great mansion. But he walked in the other direction along a wide passageway which ended in two huge double-doors.

Clint Wilbur opened them and they walked into what was the most enormous room Alita had ever seen.

"What do you think this was built for?" he asked.

She looked round.

The room was octagonal in shape, very wide, and filled with seats. There was a Gallery which would also hold a large number of people, and a stage at the far end.

The windows were all high up near the roof and she realised that the whole room was an addition to the house and not part of the original design.

"It must be a Theatre ..." she began, looking in a puzzled way at the seats.

Clint Wilbur did not speak, then after a moment she said in a different voice:

"I suppose you know it would make the most magnificent Riding-School?"

She saw by the expression on his face that that was exactly what he had been expecting her to say.

"You thought of that too!" she exclaimed.

"It had occurred to me."

"But you must see for yourself how easy it would be to clear out all these chairs and have a door where the stage is for the horses to come in from outside. The balcony could hold the spectators, and you could instal six or seven jumps."

Alita spoke in an excited manner.

She remembered that she had seen a Riding-School a long time ago in London.

She had only been ten at the time and had been with her father in the Park.

They had met a friend of his, who had said:

"I am just off to see 'Skittles' break in a new horse. Why not come with me, Harry? Watching that woman is more exciting than seeing a dozen pretty dancers perform at Covent Garden."

"I agree with you," Alita's father had said, "but..."

He had hesitated and looked at her.

"It will do the child good," his friend replied without him asking the question. "If she is going to be a horse-woman, she had better start by seeing the best!"

They had gone to a Riding-School which was somewhere in Belgravia and found half-a-dozen of her father's friends there. They were all gentlemen who made a fuss of her and told her she was a pretty child.

They had sat in the balcony and watched a woman who, with the grace of a Queen, was breaking in a wild horse with severity and yet with an expertise that Alita had known was remarkable.

Many years later she had seen her mother's frown when her father mentioned the name Skittles, and she had learnt that the woman she had watched had been Catherine Walters, not only the most notable woman-rider in the country but also the most notorious courtesan.

Ladies either pretended never to have heard of her or shuddered when her name was mentioned; but she was the only woman in England to jump the eighteen-foot water-jump at the National Hunt Steeplechase at Market Harborough.

Alita could remember all too vividly that while she had the face of an angel, when her horse had funked a jump she had sworn at it in a manner which had left Alita wide-eyed with astonishment.

Her father and his friends, however, had laughed as if it were a familiar joke which they found very funny.

The Riding-School at Marshfield would be considerably bigger than the one where Alita had seen Skittles perform, and she knew that if anybody could make good use of it, it would be Clint Wilbur.

"You must do it!" she cried. "Imagine riding King Hal here when it is frosty and the ground is too hard to jump him outside."

Her eyes were on the centre of the floor as she said:

"Wild West would soon learn, I am sure, to take one fence quickly after another. It is only a question of timing."

She was speaking as if to herself, and she smiled apologetically as she said:

"There is no need for me to explain that to you."

"And what about Flamingo?" Clint Wilbur asked.

"I would love to bring him over sometime when no-one is here. I expect you will go back to London several times a month, especially if it is too frosty to hunt."

"I have an idea that I want to talk about to you," Clint Wilbur said, "but we can do it more comfortably in the Library, which I am sure is the background you prefer."

Barbara Cartland

He spoke almost mockingly, but Alita was only too happy to follow him through the great pillared marble Hall to where she knew the Library was situated.

As they went she was astounded by what had been done already.

Because the late owner had been ill for some time before he died, the house had grown shabby. His children, even before they heard the will, were aware that they would not be able to live at Marshfield and therefore had wasted no money on redecoration.

Now there were dozens of men in every room Alita passed, working on the walls, cleaning the exquisitely painted ceilings, and reupholstering the furniture.

She stared about her in astonishment, finding it almost unbelievable that so much had been put in hand so quickly.

Clint Wilbur did not say anything but led Alita into the Library, which she saw had not been touched.

She was glad, because she liked the books which filled the walls from floor to ceiling and the worn red leather sofa and arm-chairs which she had always thought were very masculine.

There was a fire burning in the grate and Clint Wilbur indicated a chair beside it.

"What would you like to drink?" he asked. "I suggest a glass of champagne. I feel we should celebrate..."

Before she could ask the question, he finished:

"Our partnership, if that is the right word! And I would like to thank you for helping me with the stables and for confirming my impression that the Music-Room is a waste of space."

"Is that what it was built for?" Alita asked. "I do not remember having heard of concerts ever being given there."

"The Agent explained to me that it was added about sixty years ago by the owner's father."

"He must have been very musical," Alita said with a smile, "but I feel that your horses would make better use of it."

"They are not my horses yet."

He rang a bell and when a servant appeared he merely said:

"Champagne!"

"Very good, Sir."

The servant closed the door and Clint Wilbur stood in front of the fire.

"Now, what is your starting price?" he asked.

Alita drew a deep breath.

"The Duke ... suggested a thousand guineas each."

"And you expect me to pay that, knowing that the market value is about five hundred guineas for the best of them?"

"They are all good!" she flashed.

"Very well—five hundred guineas each."

"I think they are worth more. As you know yourself, the fact that we have such an excellent racecourse to train them on has added enormously to their capabilites and so to their value."

Alita spoke earnestly, but she felt a little embarrassed because Clint Wilbur was looking at her in what she thought was a cynical manner.

It was as if he knew that because he was rich he was expected to pay more than anyone else would have to pay.

"What you have to ... consider," Alita said with an effort, "is that you might pick up as good ... if not better, although I doubt it ... by going farther afield. But that will take time, and perhaps you would have difficulties of transport, while the Duke's stables are to hand. In fact, one only has to ride from one field to another."

"That is something I have already taken into consideration," Clint Wilbur replied.

She knew he was laughing at her and she thought that it was ignominious to have to bargain and fight over horses that she did not even own.

She had spent so much time on them and they had meant so much to her that she knew that when she had to part with them it would be agonising in a way that only another horse-lover would understand.

She had a sudden longing to say to Clint Wilbur: "Very well, if they are worth so little to you, leave them alone."

But she knew she could not go back to the Castle and tell her uncle that she had failed and he could not have the money on which he had set his heart.

Clint Wilbur was watching her as if he knew what she was thinking, and before either of them could speak the Butler returned.

With him was a footman carrying a silver tray and on it was an ice-bucket in which reposed an already opened bottle of champagne.

The golden wine was poured into two glasses and Alita took hers tentatively.

It was a long time since she had drunk alcohol of any sort and she hoped it would not prevent her from having a clear head and being able to continue her argument.

The servants put the tray down on a side-table.

"Is there anything else you require, Sir?" the Butler asked.

"No, thank you," Clint Wilbur replied.

Only as the door shut did he say to Alita:

"Perhaps you would have preferred tea? I forgot I was in England, and tea at four o'clock is a sacred institution."

"I cannot stay long," Alita answered. "I must get back to the Castle and help Sam with the horses."

"And you would like a decision before you leave?"

The Race for Love

"Yes, please."

"Then I will tell you what I will do," he said. "I will split the difference between us. I will pay seven hundred fifty guineas for each horse, on two conditions."

"More conditions?" Alita murmured.

"They are a habit of mine."

"What are ... they?"

"First, that the Duke will keep the horses until the renovation of my stables, which you will supervise day by day, is complete."

"Day by day?"

"It is your design, your plan. You must see that Durrant carries out your instructions."

Alita wondered what the Duke would say if he realised that she was to go to Marshfield House every day. Then she told herself that seven hundred fifty guineas was a fabulous price for the horses and he would not be likely to squabble over the details.

"And the other condition?" she asked.

"It concerns you."

"Me?"

"When you said just now that the Music-Room would make an excellent Riding-School, I had an idea."

Alita wondered what it could be, but she did not speak and Clint Wilbur went on:

"In America I was very interested in the Theatre. I have backed one or two Shows, which, as it happens, have been unqualified successes."

Alita thought to herself that they were bound to be! She was certain that everything he touched would be successful, and besides, as her father had said often enough, "Money always goes to money."

"One thing I have never done," Clint Wilbur went on, "is to stage a performance of live animals. I do not like Circuses, but an Exhibition of horsemanship is something very different."

"Like the Spanish Riding-School in Vienna?"

"Exactly!"

"I am sure it would be very exciting!"

"I think so," he agreed. "And of course the star of the Show would be Flamingo."

"Flamingo?" she replied.

"He can do the tricks you demonstrated to me and any others I have not yet seen."

"You are ... suggesting that I should ... ride him?"

"Who else?"

"That is impossible! Quite impossible!"

"Why?"

"Because my ..."

She was going to say: "my uncle would never allow it," but she managed to bite back the words before they fell from her lips.

"I am sorry to ... refuse you," she said, "but I could ... never do anything like ... that."

She thought he looked disappointed, and she added quickly:

"But I am sure I could teach you how to handle Flamingo."

"I doubt it," Clint Wilbur replied. "He is your horse, and he not only hears what you say but knows what you are thinking."

Alita thought wildly that that was true. At the same time, Clint Wilbur must be crazy if he thought she could appear in any performance he might stage.

"Let me explain what I want to do," he said. "A friend of mine, an American, is playing the leading part at the Gaiety Theatre in London."

"The Gaiety?"

"I expect you know all about it," he said with a note of amusement in his voice. "I understand it is one of the great British institutions."

That was true enough.

Alita had heard about the Gaiety Theatre from her father, from her Cousin Gerald, and from the newspapers that she read assiduously in an effort to keep in touch with the world that still existed outside the Castle.

The Gaiety was the most famous Variety Theatre in the world, and her father had always promised that as soon as she was old enough he would take her there to see a Musical Burlesque.

He had told her that they had been described by the owner of the Theatre, a man called Hollingshead, with a slogan which became famous: "The Sacred Lamp of Burlesque."

Whenever people spoke of the Gaiety there seemed to be a sparkle in their eyes and a smile on their lips.

It had for Alita always personified music, dancing feet, and bright lights.

She had known when she came to live at the Castle that all those things would be denied to her for the rest of her life.

Because like so much else they were out of reach, she had followed the different Shows at the Gaiety with the same interest that she accorded to the political news and to the foreign countries she read about in her uncle's Library.

She knew, for instance, that the Gaiety Girls were the most beautiful that could be found anywhere on the stage and that they were also the embodiment of elegance.

She had once asked her father about them and he had said:

"For a young, unmarried man to take a Gaiety Girl out to supper and drive her home in a hansom is the most exciting thing he could do."

"But why are they different from any other women, Papa?" Alita had enquired.

"I think," he had replied, "it is because they personify not only beauty but laughter and fun. We all need fun, Alita, as you will find as you grow older."

He had spoken sadly and she knew that something personal was troubling him, but she was too shy to ask him what it was.

The Gaiety fascinated her, and when she read

about the Shows put on there she found that the critics became more and more enthusiastic about every new Burlesque.

There had been *Our Cinderella; Galatea, or Pygmalion Reversed; Camaralzaman; Our Helen; Very Little Hamlet; Mezeppa;* and *The Vicar of Wide-Awake Field.*

She loved their names and she loved reading about the people who performed in them.

She therefore knew that Miss Wadman, an American who for some unknown reason was never billed as having a Christian name, was a favourite with the public because of her voice, her good acting, and her lovely appearance.

The expression on her face must have told Clint Wilbur that she knew who he was talking about.

"I see you have heard of Miss Wadman."

"Yes."

"I am giving a party for her," he said, "and also for Nellie Farren."

"Nellie Farren!"

Alita cried out the name.

"You mean she is coming ... here? To ... stay?"

"Only for two nights," Clint Wilbur replied, "but the Show she is in at the moment will soon be taken off. They are to stage a new one, called *Little Jack Sheppard,* at the end of the year."

"I read about that!" Alita exclaimed.

"Well, Nellie and my friend Miss Wadman will be arriving after the Saturday-night performance and will stay until Monday afternoon. I promised them I would provide something exceptional, but I was not certain what it would be until now."

"You mean that you will put on a ... Show for ... them in the Riding-School?"

"That is what I have been saying," Clint Wilbur said, "and you and Flamingo will be the leading actors, just as Nellie and Miss Wadman are leading actresses at the Gaiety."

Alita gave a little sigh.

"It is a wonderful idea, but impossible! Absolutely impossible!"

"Nothing is impossible!" Clint Wilbur replied. "And, as it happens, if you do not want the Duke to know what you are doing, it is very possible."

"How?"

"Because the Duke told me last night at dinner that he, the Duchess, and Lady Hermione are all invited to stay at Windsor Castle at the time that Nellie Farren and Miss Wadman will be staying here."

Alita stared at him wide-eyed.

It flashed through her mind that if he was entertaining ladies from the Gaiety, surely none of her aunt's friends in the County would be among the guests.

Then she told herself that she must be mad to consider such a thing for one moment. How could she, the Duke's niece, perform in public? And what was more, she would look a fine figure of fun in front of the beautiful and exquisitely dressed leading-ladies from the Gaiety.

She took a little sip of her champagne and put it down on the table beside her.

"I am sure you will give Miss Farren and Miss Wadman a treat," she said, "and I would love to be able to see it, but it is something I cannot do. However, I will ... lend you ... Flamingo."

Clint Wilbur did not speak for a moment, and Alita looking up at him, felt a little tremor of fear.

There was something in the squareness of his chin and the tightness of his lips which told her that he was going to be difficult.

"I am ... sorry," she said again.

"So am I," he answered, "but, as you suggest, I dare say I shall be able to handle Flamingo. Of course in those circumstances I shall expect him to be included in the deal with the other horses."

Barbara Cartland

Alita felt as if her heart had stopped beating, and she stared at him incredulously.

"Y-you... do not... mean that?" she asked. "You ... cannot mean it! You promised... you would not ... suggest such a thing!"

"I told you I always have my own way," Clint Wilbur replied. "If you will not agree to show Flamingo to my friends, then I must do it myself, and naturally I could not waste time learning how to handle a horse unless he belonged to me."

"B-but he is... mine!" Alita said passionately.

"I daresay the Duke will provide you with another mount," Clint Wilbur answered casually. "Will you inform His Grace that I will buy Flamingo as well as those he showed me this morning?"

He moved as if to escort her to the door, but, with her fingers locked together, Alita could only look at him, her grey eyes seeming to fill the whole of her small face.

"Please... listen to me," she begged.

"There is really nothing to discuss," he answered, "and I dislike arguments."

"I... told you, Flamingo is... all I have in the ... whole world.... How can he matter to you when you... have so much?"

"I do not have a horse to equal him in intelligence or who can give such a unique performance."

"E-even... if I... said I would... do it," Alita said desperately, "do you... realise that I have n-nothing to... wear except... what I have on? Of course, I would be a clown for your... friends to... laugh at.... Perhaps that is what you... intend?"

"If you take part in my Show," Clint Wilbur said coldly, "I will naturally provide, as any Theatrical Manager expects to do, the right clothes for the performance."

"I... I could not... let you... do that."

"Why not?"

"It would be... wrong and... improper... for a

gentleman to... p-pay for what a... lady wears."

"I am not asking you to appear as a lady," Clint Wilbur retorted, "but as a rider. That, as you must admit, is a very different thing."

He had the answer to everything, Alita thought, and yet how could she possibly do what he asked?

But she could not lose Flamingo... she could not! He was the only thing left in her life, and, as she had already said, perhaps indiscreetly, the only being who loved her and whom she really loved.

After all, she asked herself, what did it matter if she did something unconventional?

It would doubtless horrify her uncle and aunt if they should ever learn of it. But they would never in their wildest dreams imagine her behaving in such a way.

The alternative to doing what Mr. Wilbur asked of her was to sit alone in the Castle as she had done for three years, which seemed like three centuries, with no-one to talk to, no-one even to notice her except with contempt and dislike.

To lose Flamingo would be to lose her last touch with the life she had once known and her last memories of happiness.

She felt that Clint Wilbur was impatiently waiting for her to leave and she felt too that what decision she came to was really a matter of indifference to him.

He wanted her to do as he wished. If she refused, he would manage without her, perhaps even find another woman to take her place on Flamingo's back.

She could not bear it. It was too much! She knew that without Flamingo she would only want to die!

"Very... well," she said in a strange little voice that seemed to come from a long way away. "I will... do what you... ask."

Chapter Four

Riding towards Marshfield House, Alita felt her heart still pounding from the altercation she had just had with her uncle.

The Duchess and Hermione had been to a dinner-party the night before, and when Alita entered the Breakfast-Room she found only her uncle sitting at the table.

"Good-morning, Uncle Lionel!" she said. "I am sorry to be late, but Sam was worried about Sparkling Knight's fetlock."

The Duke only grunted, and as Alita sat down a footman offered her a dish of bacon and eggs.

She was feeling rather breathless as she had run up the three flights of stairs to her bed-room to pull off her habit and hurry into the first gown she found, buttoning it up at the back as she ran back downstairs.

The Duke did not speak until the servants had left the room. Then he raised his eyes from *The Times* to say:

"It is time, Alita, that you stopped all this nonsense of spending so much time at Marshfield House."

Alita put down her knife and fork to stare at him in consternation before she answered:

"What . . . do you mean . . . Uncle Lionel?"

"You can understand English, I suppose?" the Duke retorted sharply. "Your aunt has found out that you spend much time in that man's stables, and she considers it quite unnecessary. What is more, it is likely to cause gossip."

"There is no chance of that, Uncle Lionel," Alita said quickly. "But Mr. Wilbur insists that I superintend the alterations to the stables. They are nearly finished, and then our horses can move in there."

"I agree with your aunt that your supervision is quite ridiculous!" the Duke replied angrily. "I admit you brought off a good deal for me with Wilbur, and I shall be delighted when I have the cheque in my hand. In the meantime, you stay here. Do you understand?"

"Mr. Wilbur made my . . . assistance in the . . . alterations to his . . . stables a . . . condition of . . . the sale," Alita said falteringly.

Her uncle brought his fist down angrily on the table, making the china and the silver rattle.

"I have never heard such impertinence!" he stormed. "Let me make it quite clear, I will not be dictated to by an American, however rich he may be!"

He paused before he said firmly:

"You can tell Wilbur for me today that this is the last time you will go to the Marshfield stables. Is that clear?"

Alita was sure from the way her uncle was talking that the Duchess must have made an issue of the whole matter to arouse him to such a state of anger.

She suspected that the reason was that Mr. Wilbur had not paid court to Hermione as they had hoped and indeed expected.

She knew that her uncle and aunt had given a large party for him to meet the County, but, from what Hermione had told her afterwards, while he had been polite and charming to everybody, he had not singled her out in any way.

Nor had he shown any more interest in her at other times, as when he came to the Castle or they met outside, than he had shown the first day they had met.

In a way it was absurd that the Duke should have set his heart on having Clint Wilbur as a son-in-law.

Alita was quite certain that when they got to know each other better, they would find that apart from horses they had little in common.

She realised, meeting Clint Wilbur every day, that he had an astute, intelligent mind which made him knowledgeable about a great many things of which her uncle was supremely ignorant.

He was also even more autocratic than the Duke.

She could well imagine that if the two men were together for any length of time, not only would they disagree on a great number of subjects, but also their personalities would come into violent conflict.

She knew now with a sense of dismay that Clint Wilbur would be furious at having his plans circumvented, while at the same time it would be extremely difficult for her to defy her uncle.

As if he felt slightly apologetic at having been so violent, he said more gently:

"Surely those damned stables are finished by now? I could have built an Army Barracks in the time you have been going over there!"

"It is only a little over a week, Uncle Lionel."

She spoke humbly, in what she thought was a conciliatory tone, but the Duke once aroused was difficult to pacify.

"In the meantime, our horses are being neglected," he said. "I know you sold the bulk of them to Wilbur, but there are the mares and foals, and I have learnt that one which was born yesterday is dead, I presume from neglect!"

"That is not fair, Uncle Lionel," Alita retorted. "Sam suspected that the foal was not in the right position. It was born with a twisted neck and it was really best that it did not live."

"You are making excuses!" the Duke roared. "If you had been there as you should have been it would doubtless have survived. I will have no more of it, Alita, and that is an order!"

He threw *The Times* down on the floor and rose from the breakfast-table.

"Inform Mr. Wilbur of my decision, and tell him I require your services here at the Castle!"

The Duke turned and walked from the room, closing the door sharply behind him.

Alita stared after him in consternation.

She was quite sure that if her uncle was angry, Clint Wilbur would be angrier still, and she thought with a sigh that she had in fact been fortunate that all this had not occurred sooner.

She had been well aware that if the Duchess had had the slightest intimation that she was spending so much time at Marshfield House she would have interfered immediately.

There was no use pleading that Clint Wilbur had no idea who she was, trying to convince her aunt and uncle that he treated her in exactly the same way as he treated his architect and the other people he employed.

Actually, however, this was not quite true.

She and Clint Wilbur had had long consultations together about the progress that was being made in the Riding-School, and what fortunately had gone unnoticed was that he rode nearly every morning with her on the race-course.

She was usually there before he appeared, so that she could teach Flamingo some new tricks and take him through his repertoire of old ones.

She acknowledged to herself that she looked forward eagerly and with a strange excitement to the moment when she would see a man riding out of the morning mist as if he stepped out from a magical world to enter into her own.

Everything at Marshfield House did seem magical.

Clint Wilbur was transforming it into what it must have looked like when it had first been built.

The beautiful ceilings glowed with colour which had been obscured by the dirt and dust of ages; and the gold-leaf on the cornices, which also decorated much of the white panelling, shone with a pristine brilliance.

And apart from the fine furniture which had belonged to the house originally, Clint Wilbur was bringing in new treasures.

Art Dealers came down from London with paintings that he chose with a discrimination and faultless good taste that Alita found surprising.

She had not expected an American to know so much about painting, furniture, and china, but she was sure that Clint Wilbur was a very unusual American.

As he had said himself, his Cosmopolitan education was certainly different from that available to the majority of his countrymen.

He showed Alita his new purchases as he accumulated them and let her look at the rooms as they progressed under the decorator's hands.

This was a delight which made her feel for the first time in three years that she was a real person, with thoughts and opinions which were of interest to somebody else.

After being snubbed, ignored, and treated with contempt, it was such a change that she felt as if she had stepped out from the darkness of a fog and into the sunlight.

She counted the hours until it was time for her to

take the horses back into their stables at the Castle and ride off alone to Marshfield House.

She never presumed on Clint Wilbur's kindness but would go straight to the stables to talk to the workmen, to suggest small improvements and to approve what they had already completed.

Then she would hear his footsteps coming towards her and recognise them with a sudden leap of her heart before she turned round.

The only time she felt embarrassed was on the second day after she had agreed to perform with Flamingo in the Riding-School, when he had said as they walked towards the house:

"You will find a tailor waiting for you in one of the bed-rooms. The Housekeeper will show you which one."

"A ... tailor?" she questioned.

"I have told him what I require, and when he has finished, Maxwell of Dover Street will fit your boots."

Alita felt the colour rise in her cheeks.

He spoke casually; yet somehow it was shocking that any man should provide her with clothes, and she knew how horrified her mother would have been at the idea.

They walked on in silence, and when they reached the foot of the Grand Staircase, Clint Wilbur said:

"When you have finished you will find me in the Green Salon. I have something to show you."

She left him without a word, and the Housekeeper, waiting at the top of the stairs, escorted her to one of the magnificent State bed-rooms.

As soon as Alita heard the tailor's name she knew he was the most exclusive and certainly the most expensive cutter of riding-habits in the whole country.

He left her in no doubt as to how important he was.

"You have a figure, Miss, as good as that of Her Majesty the Empress of Austria," he said when he had taken her measurements.

"I said to her when I was making her a new habit: 'I don't believe, Your Majesty, that in the whole length of Britain there is any lady with a waist as small as yours.'"

He looked at his tape-measure in amazement as if he thought it was deceiving him, then went on:

"Believe it or not, I was wrong! Your waist, Miss, is just under eighteen inches, and that's a fraction smaller than Her Majesty's!"

"I wish I could ride as well as the Empress," Alita said with a smile.

"Ah, well, Miss, that's another thing altogether!" the tailor replied. "They tells me there's no-one to touch her in the whole of Europe, and, horses or no horses, she's the most beautiful lady I've ever seen in me whole life!"

Alita thought how she would have loved to see the Empress ride.

The stories of her amazing feats of endurance when hunting with the Quorn had been the talk of everybody who was interested in hunting.

The Duke, who had met her at Windsor Castle, had extolled her beauty and her grace with so much enthusiasm that he had made the Duchess's eyes harden and her lips tighten.

Mr. Maxwell of Dover Street, whose boots were famous and whose firm had served the great Duke of Wellington, paid Alita a different compliment.

He looked so disparagingly at the boots he drew from her feet that she had thought for one moment he would refuse to make a pair of his own to replace them.

But when he saw her legs he exclaimed:

"You have, if I may say so, Miss, a perfect leg for a boot! It's a shame, a crying shame, that they

The Race for Love

should be concealed in objects that are fit only for a bonfire!"

"I agree with you," Alita said with a smile, "but I am afraid I grew out of my old boots, and these had belonged to somebody else."

"They're too big for you, Miss, for one thing," Mr. Maxwell said.

They were like everything else that had belonged to Hermione, Alita knew: too big and invariably unbecoming.

Neither the tailor nor Mr. Maxwell quibbled at what Alita knew had to be a very rushed job if they were to be ready for her to wear in less than a fortnight's time.

She was certain that Clint Wilbur had forced them to accede to his wishes in the manner in which he always, as he himself said, got what he wanted.

There was a woman with the tailor, who stood in the background and made no comment while Alita's measurements were being taken.

She looked rather superior to be an assistant, and Alita thought that perhaps she was there only for reasons of propriety, since she was being measured by a man.

When both the tailor and Mr. Maxwell had completed what they wished to do, they bowed and went from the bed-room, and Alita was just about to follow them when the Housekeeper opened the door to announce:

"The Milliner, Miss!"

When she looked round in surprise she saw a woman come into the room carrying two round leather hat-boxes, followed by a footman with two others.

"Good-morning!" Alita said. "I am afraid I had forgotten that I would need a hat to go with my habit!"

"Two hats, Miss," the Milliner replied.

"Two?" Alita questioned. "I think there must be some mistake."

"No, Miss. One in black is what has been ordered, and one in grey."

Alita was surprised, but she thought it would be tactless to question the Milliner further, so she sat down at the dressing-table to look at herself apprehensively; her hair, as usual, very untidy.

'There is too much of it,' she thought. 'If it were not so soft, perhaps it would keep in place.'

With a little pang she remembered her father saying once as he stroked her hair:

"It is like your mother's, as soft as silk. I have always told her that it has a fairy-like quality which is different from any other woman I have ever known."

"There is certainly nothing fairy-like about its appearance now,' Alita thought despairingly.

However, the Milliner took off the loose, untidy chignon and as Alita's hair fell about her shoulders he said:

"I think, Miss, if you'll excuse me saying so, you're using too much soap on your hair, and if you use the yoke of one or two eggs as a rinse it'll give it more stamina and certainly bring out the lights in a way that's quite surprising."

"Thank you," Alita replied. "I have never heard of that before."

"I suggested it to Miss Catherine Walters many years ago," the Milliner went on, "not that I should mention her name to you, Miss, but she's always acclaimed for her appearance on a horse, and many's the time she's thanked me for the difference I've made to her hair."

"I will certainly remember what you have said," Alita answered, remembering how she had seen the famous Skittles breaking in a horse.

The Milliner arranged her hair in a tidy bun; then, opening her hat-boxes, he brought out what

Alita knew was the very latest high-crowned black riding-hat.

It was draped with a gauze veil which hung down behind, and the moment she tried it on she saw how very different she looked.

"A little too big, Miss," the Milliner said, and produced another, identical hat, but which fitted Alita perfectly.

"Of course it will look very different when you have on a smart habit, Miss," the Milliner said with a disdainful glance at Alita's threadbare jacket. "I understand that you are to wear the bodice-habit which is worn by Her Majesty the Empress."

"Oh, am I?" Alita exclaimed. "How exciting!"

She knew the bodice-habit was very much smarter than the jacket and skirt.

It fitted closely to the figure and it was well known that the Empress was always sewn into her habit before she went hunting to make it tighter still.

The Milliner took the hat from Alita's head and opened another hat-box to bring out one that was almost identical with the former but in grey.

It was not the hard ugly grey that Alita always associated in her mind with charity children, but the soft blue-grey of a pigeon's breast-feathers.

When it was on her head it seemed to blend with the strange ash colour of her hair, and yet at the same time it accentuated the golden tones that she had almost forgotten were there.

"Charming!" the Milliner said. "And I am making the veil a little longer, Miss, to almost reach the shoulders; it looks very graceful that way, especially when you're moving."

'It will move when I jump!' Alita thought to herself, but aloud she said:

"It looks very attractive. Thank you."

"I think the grey habit will suit you even better than the black one, Miss," the Milliner said. "But

Barbara Cartland

then, if you'll excuse me saying so, I'm sure you'll 'pay with dressing,' as the saying goes."

"I doubt it," Alita replied almost to herself.

At the same time, she could not help feeling the excitement that every woman feels when it is a question of wearing beautiful and expensive clothes.

Nothing could be more thrilling than to have a habit made by a master-tailor and hats in which she looked very different from the bedraggled creature who wore a jockey-cap because it would stay on her head as she exercised the horses.

'It will certainly be a one-night Show,' she thought to herself, 'then, having played a leading part, once and for all I shall leave the Theatre forever!'

It would however give her something to remember, something perhaps to dream about in the long years that lay ahead.

Because it was so depressing to think of them, she had run downstairs quickly to find Clint Wilbur and not miss one passing second of the new and thrilling experiences that knowing him had brought her.

He had a picture to show her and he asked her opinion as to whether she thought it should hang over the mantelpiece in the Green Salon.

It was a very beautiful picture by Turner of a sunrise, with great bursts of colour, yellow, orange, and crimson, that seemed to bring new light to the predominately green Salon.

"Do you like it?" Clint Wilbur asked.

"I think it is lovely!" Alita answered. "It is so clever of you to be aware that this was what the room needed."

Without realising that it might sound impertinent, she asked:

"How do you know these thing? How can you be so knowledgeable about art as well as horses?"

"It is not particularly complimentary that you should be surprised," he replied.

"I am ... sorry," she answered. "I did not ... mean to be ... rude. It is just that most men have one particular interest and their horizons do not extend any farther."

"And you think I am different?"

"Of course you are!" she answered. "Since I have known you we have talked of so many different subjects, and it is very wonderful for me in a way that I cannot ... explain."

"Why not?" he asked.

She started at his question, feeling that she had been indiscreet in referring to herself.

She did not speak and after a moment he said:

"I asked you a question. Why should you not explain to me why it means so much to you that we should talk of these things?"

He paused for a moment, then went on:

"Sometimes when we are talking I see an expression in your eyes that is almost one of hunger, as if you have been starved mentally and spiritually. Is that true?"

"Y-yes!" Alita said after a moment. "But I do not ... want to talk about it. Please ... tell me where you found this picture ... I am sure it was extremely lucky that you should have discovered it just at the right moment."

"We were talking about you!"

She was afraid of the note in his voice, knowing that if he was determined to make her speak of things that must be kept secret, it would be very hard to circumvent him.

She glanced at the clock and gave an exclamation.

"I must go!" she said. "I should have been back at the Castle half-an-hour ago."

"You are running away," he accused her. "I have a very good mind to stop you."

"If you do I might not be able to come tomorrow," she replied.

Then she had run from the room before he could prevent her.

She had not been speaking seriously, but now, riding towards Marshfield House, Alita knew that always at the back of her mind there had been the fear that the joy and excitement that Clint Wilbur gave her would come to an end.

Then she would be a prisoner again in the Castle, moving like a ghost about the rooms, ready to disappear if anybody should call unexpectedly.

"It was too good to last," Alita told herself.

But that did not prevent her from feeling an ache within her breast that was a physical pain.

There was only one consolation. At the end of this week her uncle, her aunt, and her cousin Hermione would all be leaving for Windsor Castle and there would be nobody to stop her from taking part in Clint Wilbur's production in the Riding-School.

She only hoped he would not be too angry that she could not come to him before then; that he would refuse to buy her uncle's horses as he had agreed to do; worse, that he would punish her by including Flamingo amongst the others, despite the fact that she had agreed to do what he wished.

When she reached Marshfield House it was difficult to concentrate on the last few things that were being finished off in the stables and to congratulate Mr. Durrant and his workmen with the enthusiasm they obviously expected from her.

There was no doubt that the work in the stables had been well carried out.

Alita was sure that there was no stable in the whole County, or in any other, which was more up-to-date or which catered in every possible way for the comfort of its occupants.

She knew that Clint Wilbur's grooms were delighted with what had been achieved, and the horses he already owned had been moved into the altered stalls and seemed to appreciate their new surroundings.

Alita was talking to the Head-groom and giving him the names of the horses that were to come from the Castle so that they could be inscribed above each of their mangers, when she heard the step she always recognised.

Clint Wilbur came to her side.

"Good-morning, Miss Blair!"

They had already ridden together at six o'clock that morning on the race-course, but he always came there alone and she knew that his grooms had no idea that they met.

"Good-morning, Mr. Wilbur," she replied demurely.

"I see the stables are nearly completed," he said, "but we have a snag in the Riding-School on which I would like your advice."

He walked across the yard, and a little way beyond the stables they reached the new doors which had been erected as an entrance to the Riding-School.

They were open, and as together they walked through them Alita looked with delight at the transformation that had been made since they had first agreed upon what should be done.

"We decided that there should be seven fences," Clint Wilbur was saying, "and I am wondering if there is really enough space for a horse to recover his balance after taking fence three before he gets himself into position for number four."

Alita walked across the newly laid down floor to inspect it.

"I think King Hal and Flamingo could do it," she said, "but I am not certain about the others."

She looked round and added:

"I realise what is wrong: the corner is too sharp. If we move the fence at the end, there could be a space of several more feet between fences three and four."

"You are right!" Clint Wilbur exclaimed. "I cannot think why I did not realise that myself!"

He gave the order; then he said to Alita:

"I think the sooner you bring your horses over here the better. Then we can have a chance to try them out in the Riding-School. Of course it is essential that they should rehearse what they have to do before the Opening Night."

He smiled as he spoke, but Alita said in a low voice:

"I have ... something to ... tell you."

"What is it?"

They left the Riding-School through the door which led into the house, and walked towards the Library as they had done so often before.

They reached it, and as Clint Wilbur shut the door behind them Alita said:

"I ... I am afraid you may be ... angry at what I have to say ... to you."

"I will try not to be," he replied. "What has happened?"

"The Duke has ... forbidden me to come ... here after ... today."

"Why?"

"The Duchess has found out that I have been advising you about the stables."

"Why should it perturb her?"

Alita knew this was a difficult question, and she thought quickly.

"Both the Duke and the Duchess have been very ... kind to me since I have been at the Castle, and... I... I think they have my... well-being at ... heart."

"I can understand that," Clint Wilbur replied. "At the same time, the Duke has made it quite clear what your position is in his stables."

Alita did not answer and there was a silence between them before he said:

"How much does His Grace pay you?"

The question was unexpected and Alita looked at him in a frightened manner before she replied:

"That is... immaterial.... He feeds me and gives me a... roof over my head."

"Are you telling me that you receive no salary?"

Alita wanted to lie, to say that she was paid a weekly wage like everybody else; but then she thought, seeing her appearance, that it would be difficult for Clint Wilbur to believe that she had any money to spend.

Therefore, she said quickly:

"I... I am sorry... but the Duke was very... emphatic that I was neglecting my duties at the Castle by... coming here so often."

"I was going to suggest that whatever salary you are paid, I will double or even treble it, but as it appears that you have a very different arrangement, let me make another suggestion."

He paused before he said slowly:

"I will give you a house on the Estate, Miss Blair, and I will pay you the wage I think you are worth, which is a very high one, if you will terminate your employment with the Duke and come and work for me."

Alita was so astonished that she could only stare at him wide-eyed, then finally she said:

"No... no... it is very... kind of you... but I cannot... do that."

"Why not?"

There was a hard note in his voice and she knew it was the usual prelude to a battle in which he was determined to have his own way.

She thought wildly what she should say.

"The... the Duke is... is my... Guardian," she said at length, a little incoherently. "When my... father died... I was left in his... care."

"Your Guardian!" Clint Wilbur exclaimed in surprise. "He seems a strange sort of Guardian to me, Miss Blair, seeing the way he lets you dress and the manner in which you work apparently without any recompense."

"It... it is... an arrangement which I... cannot break."

"Nonsense!" Clint Wilbur retorted. "You are entitled to live your life as you wish to do; and seeing how you care so well for the horses you have trained for him, I cannot believe that you would not be happier continuing with them than starting again from scratch."

He paused for a moment as if he was thinking. Then he went on:

"I have already decided to extend my activities, and I shall require much bigger stables for the horses I intend to buy."

He knew that Alita was listening as he went on:

"So far we have concentrated on Steeplechasing, but why should I not enter for the Flat Races? I have rather set my heart on winning the Derby!"

Alita drew in her breath.

Then, with a smile which she felt almost hypnotised her, he added:

"I need your help and your advice to make me sure of being first past the winning-post."

Alita had an incredible feeling that if they could do it together it would be possible. Then with an effort she said:

"I am sorry... more sorry than I can... say, that I have to... do as the Duke... wishes."

"And suppose I will not let you?" Clint Wilbur asked.

She did not answer, and his voice was suddenly angry as he said:

"Must you always be so obstinate and try to prevent me from getting what I want? I need your help. I want to buy horses, dozens of horses; I want to breed from them to build up a racing-stable which will rival any I have seen or heard about in this country. Dammitall, most women would be thrilled to be offered such an assignment! Why should you be the one exception?"

There was a note of anger in his voice that seemed to Alita to vibrate round the room and through her.

Then the pain that had been in her breast ever since her uncle had raged at her at breakfast-time, and the unhappiness that she had felt because she knew she had to obey him, seemed to intensify.

Her whole body was filled with the pain of it.

Suddenly everything blurred and darkness seemed to seep over her as with a little incoherent murmur she put out her hand to save herself from falling.

Even as she was lost in a kind of terrifying oblivion she felt strong arms lift her, and she found herself lying on the sofa with her head against a silk cushion....

She thought she was alone and that he had left her because he was angry, but then he came from a corner of the room, carrying a glass in his hand.

He put his arm round her shoulders, lifted her head, and held a glass to her lips.

"Drink this."

Vaguely, as if through a mist, she obeyed him,

Barbara Cartland

and felt a fire beginning to seep down her throat. Putting up her hand weakly, she tried to push away the glass.

"No..."

"A little more," he insisted.

Because it was impossible to refuse to do what he wished, she sipped a little more of the brandy and felt it searing through her, and then the darkness began to disappear.

"When did you last have something to eat?" Clint Wilbur asked.

With an effort Alita tried to think.

She had not eaten her breakfast because her uncle was being angry with her, and she remembered that last night when everybody had gone out she had been forgotten and it had been too much trouble to go to the kitchen and find something for herself.

"I...I am all...right"

"That is not what I asked you," Clint Wilbur said. "I am sure that because you were upset by the Duke you had no breakfast."

She was surprised that he should be so perceptive where she was concerned.

He set her head back gently on the cushion and walked to the fireplace to ring the bell.

A servant opened the door a few seconds later.

"I want breakfast for Miss Blair," Clint Wilbur said sharply. "Coffee, and dishes that can be prepared quickly."

"Very good, Sir!"

The footman shut the door and hurried away.

Clint Wilbur moved back to the sofa to stand looking down at Alita.

Her hat had fallen off when he carried her to the sofa, and when he had left her to ring the bell she had shut her eyes, fighting against her weakness and feeling that she was floating away from reality.

Now she looked up at him and said:

"I am ... sorry to be ... so foolish."

"It is very foolish to go without food," he said severely, "especially when you have been working so many hours already."

"I ... know."

"If you work for me, I promise I shall make it a condition that you have three good meals a day—and to make quite certain that you do so, I will even provide them."

He spoke with a hint of amusement in his voice and Alita thought thankfully that he was obviously no longer angry.

"Now that I look at you," he went on, "I realise that you are much too thin. What on earth do you gain by working yourself to the bone?"

"S-someone has to ... look after the ... horses," Alita murmured, feeling that he was waiting for an answer.

"So the willing horse takes on the whole burden," Clint Wilbur said cynically. "But you will be no help to anybody if you starve yourself into the grave."

"I shall not do ... that," Alita said with a smile. "It was only this ... morning because I was ... upset to think I could not ... come here any more."

"You wanted to come?"

"You ... know I do."

"Then let me talk to the Duke."

The suggestion made her struggle to sit upright.

"No ... no ... of course not! You must ... not do that. Promise me you will ... not do ... that!"

"If he is a proper sort of Guardian, he will realise that it would be to your advantage," he said slowly.

"Promise me you will not ... speak to him about ... me," Alita begged. "He would be angry ... not with you but with ... me, and it would make things more ... difficult than they are ... already."

"Why should they be difficult?"

"I cannot explain... and please do not... try to ... make me."

There was something pathetic in the way Alita pleaded with him.

She saw on his face an expression which she did not understand, before he turned away to stand with his back to her, looking down into the fire.

He did not speak for a long time and Alita looked at him anxiously, perturbed by his silence and yet afraid to say anything herself in case she should make the situation worse.

It was a great relief when the door opened and servants came in carrying a small table covered with a white linen cloth, which they set down near the fireplace.

Then other things appeared almost like magic: coffee in a silver pot with a jug of thick cream to add to it, covered dishes containing eggs, and freshly baked hot rolls and bread with golden butter made from Jersey cream.

As Alita rose a little unsteadily to walk to the chair beside the table, she thought it would be embarrassing if, after all the trouble she had caused, she was unable to eat anything.

But after she had drunk a little coffee she suddenly felt hungry and knew that it was the stimulus of the brandy that had brought back her appetite.

While she ate, Clint Wilbur sat on the red-leather-covered fire-guard seat, which was like one Alita remembered her father used to have in his Smoking-Room at home.

She always thought there was something cosy about a man sitting in front of the fire, "warming his tail" as she had heard someone describe it.

She thought with a sudden contraction of her heart that perhaps this would be the last time she would ever be in such a situation and never again with a man as attractive as Clint Wilbur.

As she finished her hot roll spread with home-made marmalade she said:

"I am... ashamed of my... behaviour. At the same time, I cannot remember when I have enjoyed a meal as much as this one."

"You are very easily pleased," Clint Wilbur answered. "The ladies I usually entertain demand caviar and champagne."

"At this moment I can think of nothing more delicious than eggs and marmalade," Alita said with a smile.

"Are you strong enough to return to the subject which upset you?" he enquired.

"N-no," she answered. "Please do not... say any more. There is nothing I can do... nothing... and I can only... beg of you to be... understanding."

"That is what I want to be," he said, "but you give me nothing to understand."

She looked unhappy, and he said:

"You leave me feeling more frustrated than I have ever been before. Problems are something I can cope with. Obstacles are only there for me to demolish them. But secrecy and silence are something quite different."

He paused, then unexpectedly put out his hand towards her.

"Trust me with whatever it is that is so obviously worrying you, and let me see if I can unravel the puzzle which is too difficult for you alone."

There was something in his voice and the kindness in his expression and his outstretched hand which made the tears come into Alita's eyes.

She told herself that it was because she was unused to kindness, because no-one ever talked to her like that nowadays, and it was years since anyone had tried to help her.

Then as she looked up at Clint Wilbur with the tears making it difficult to see him clearly, she found that everything which she wanted to say had died away on her lips.

"Trust me," he said again very quietly, and somehow, she was not certain how it happened, her hand was in his.

She felt a little tremor go through her because he was touching her. It was something she could not explain. It was almost like quicksilver running through her body.

"I want... too," she said in a very low voice, in answer to his plea. "I want to... trust you... but I cannot do so because it is not my secret... but I shall always remember how... kind you have been to me... and how happy I have been here."

His fingers tightened on hers and she thought that he was like a life-line, holding her up and sustaining her when she was sinking.

Then, with an almost superhuman effort, she told herself that she had to be sensible, had to face reality... she had to go away.

She was not certain if he drew her to her feet or if she rose by her own volition.

She only knew that she was standing beside him while he was still sitting on the fire-guard seat.

He looked at her for a long moment, then he said:

"I think you have been through enough this morning. Go back to the Castle, and for God's sake leave those horses to fend for themselves for once. Lie down and take things easy. We will talk about everything tomorrow."

"Tomorrow?" she asked.

There was a twist to his lips as he replied:

"The Duke expressly invited me to use his race-course whenever I wished."

She felt as if the sun had suddenly come out.

He was not angry, and she would see him again early in the morning, and even if she could not come to Marshfield House they would be together as they rode over the jumps.

As if he understood what she was thinking, he said gently:

"Go home and do as I say."

"You are . . . not angry?"

She knew the answer, but she wanted to hear him say it.

"Not with you."

She looked round the Library because she was seeing it for the last time.

It was such a lovely room, and now she thought that she would never be able to borrow the books, so what they contained would always be hidden from her.

Clint Wilbur picked up her hat from the floor and held it out to her.

"Stop worrying," he said. "Things have a way of solving themselves, especially when I am prodding them from behind."

"That is . . . something you . . . must not do," Alita replied, but she did not speak very positively.

Clint Wilbur did not answer. He only opened the door and they walked slowly through the house towards the door at the far end which was nearest to the stables.

As they went, Alita kept thinking:

'This is the last time . . . the last time . . .'

She felt as if even their footsteps echoed the words.

They passed the Green Salon and she wanted to ask if she could go in for one moment and look at Turner's sunrise over the mantelpiece.

Then she told herself that Clint Wilbur would not understand that she wanted to say good-bye to it.

It might even increase his determination to force her into leaving the Castle and coming to work for him.

She could imagine nothing more marvellous,

more perfect, than to accept his offer to help him increase his stable, and buy and breed horses that would win the great races of the turf.

Then she told herself that only an American would think of anything so absurd. Women did not have such a position in England and she of all women could not accept such a situation.

They reached the stables, and as soon as she appeared a groom brought Flamingo from one of the stalls.

Clint Wilbur patted the horse's neck.

"At least he has no problems," he said when Alita was ready to move off.

"On the contrary," she replied, with an effort to answer him lightly. "Flamingo is studying his cues and is quite determined to steal the limelight and all the applause."

"I am certain he will do that," Clint Wilbur answered as lightly as she had spoken. "Will you ask him whether he prefers a bouquet of carrots or a basket of apples?"

"I feel quite certain that, being so greedy, he will expect both!" Alita replied, and Clint Wilbur was laughing as she rode away.

She did not look back or she would have known that his eyes were following her as she rode out of the stable-yard and across the Park.

She was moving swiftly under the great oak trees as if she must make up for lost time by getting back to the Castle as quickly as possible.

Chapter Five

Riding towards Marshfield House on Sunday afternoon, Alita was so excited that she felt as if she could fly there through the air.

It hardly seemed possible that so much had happened in a week.

She shied away like a horse from the thought that when tonight was over everything would go back to the way it had been before Clint Wilbur came into her life.

She knew that he had not pressed her to defy the Duke and go to Marshfield House because he was aware that it would upset her.

When she got home the day after she had ignominiously fainted, she had thought that even though he had said he would see her in the morning, he might still be resentful at her refusal to tell him what he wished to know.

She had gone to the race-course apprehensively the next morning and had at first thought her worst fears were realised and he was no longer interested in her.

When as time passed and she had already taken one horse over the jumps and there was still no sign of him, she felt such an agony of disappointment that it seemed to her as if the whole world was dark and there was nothing for her now or in the future.

Then with a leap of her heart she had seen him riding through the trees and saw with surprise that he was not alone.

She had been standing with the horses which she had brought out to exercise as Clint Wilbur came towards her, another man riding beside him, who she realised rode in very much the same way as he did.

The newcomer was also tall, and as they drew nearer Alita saw that he was dressed in a somewhat eccentric manner.

The cut of his coat and his riding-breeches and the large-brimmed hat he wore on his head were certainly not conventional attire for an Englishman.

Clint Wilbur dismounted.

"Good-morning, Miss Blair!" he said. "I've brought a friend with me who is very anxious to meet you."

The man who accompanied him swung himself from the saddle, and Clint Wilbur continued:

"Let me introduce Mr. Burt Ackberg. I feel there is no need for me to explain that he also is from Texas."

If she had not known it by his appearance, Alita would have found the Texas accent unmistakable.

"Howdy, Ma'am!" he said, lifting his wide-brimmed hat. "I'm mighty glad to make your acquaintance!"

"Burt," Clint Wilbur interposed before Alita could speak, "will be the leading-man in our Show on Sunday night. He is one of the best riders I have ever seen in my life, and he does some fancy tricks on a horse which I feel sure will delight our audience."

"You sure flatter me, Clint!" Burt Ackberg protested, "and the little lady'll think I'm a regular show-off."

"Which is exactly what you are!" Clint Wilbur

said as he laughed. "And that is what Miss Blair and I require to make the evening a success."

The two men did not waste much time in talking.

Burt Ackberg inspected the horses and was undoubtedly impressed with them.

He rode over the jumps in a manner which told Alita that Clint Wilbur had not exaggerated in praising his friend's horsemanship.

Then Clint Wilbur said to Alita:

"I have a new idea for racing which I would like to suggest to you."

As he spoke he drew a stop-watch from his pocket and handed it to her, saying:

"I want you to time me exactly to the second as I take King Hal round the course. Then Burt will see if he can beat my time on Red Trump."

He mounted King Hal and rode off at what seemed to Alita to be a tremendous pace. When she clicked the watch to a stop she could hardly believe that he could have done it so quickly.

"All I can say is that back home tortoises move quicker!" Burt Ackberg teased, then set off on Red Trump, riding him as if he were a jockey, despite his height.

The result was three seconds' difference between the two men and Alita wondered if Clint Wilbur would dislike being beaten. But he only smiled and said to Alita:

"Now let us see what you can do on Rajah."

She was about to protest that she would rather ride Flamingo, when she thought that Clint Wilbur, who knew all the horses so well, had perhaps a reason for choosing Rajah as her mount.

She took him round as quickly as she could and was rather mortified when she was beaten and came in third place.

However, the men praised her and said it was excellent for a first attempt.

They tried the same sort of competition on the other horses, but it was obvious that the first three Clint Wilbur had chosen were the fastest.

When it was time for Alita to go back to the Castle, Clint Wilbur said to her:

"Look out for a surprise tomorrow morning!"

Her eyes widened and she replied:

"This morning has been very exciting! And if we are going to race again, I would like to try and see what Flamingo can do and perhaps Wild West."

"Wild West is a possibility," he replied, "but not Flamingo."

She wondered why not, then decided that it all had something to do with the Show he was planning for Sunday night, and she knew that he would not like her to be argumentative about anything.

There was also no time to linger if she was to get back to the Castle, change, and be downstairs for breakfast without incurring a reprimand and perhaps awkward questions as to why she was late.

She was certain that her uncle was determined to see that she obeyed his instructions, when he asked later in the day:

"You have told Mr. Wilbur that you will not be spending any more time at the stables at Marshfield House?"

"Yes, Uncle Lionel."

"When is he expecting the horses?"

"As soon as the stables are finished."

"Well, the sooner the better, as far as I am concerned," the Duke said.

Alita knew that he was anxious to receive Mr. Wilbur's cheque, which undoubtedly would arrive immediately after the completion of the sale.

"You have not... forgotten, Uncle Lionel," she said tentatively, "that you promised to put some money aside to buy in new horses?"

Seeing the uninterested expression on his face, she added quickly:

"As it is, Hermione will have nothing to ride this winter."

"I will let you have two thousand pounds of what Wilbur pays me," the Duke said after a moment's pause, "but not a penny more."

"Thank you, Uncle Lionel," Alita answered. "Thank you very much."

It was not a great deal, considering what he would be getting for the horses he had sold and that the stables were now depleted of anything that was rideable in the hunting-field.

Alita could not help remembering how Clint Wilbur had told her that if she worked for him she could help him not only to buy dozens of horses but to build up a racing-stable which would rival any other in the country.

Could anything, she asked herself, be a more thrilling assignment?

Then she knew that even to dream about such things was absurd and she ought to be grateful that her uncle had given her any money at all.

"Two thousand pounds!" Sam had said when she told him. "It'll not be enough, Miss Alita, for what ye wants."

"We shall just have to work hard on the yearlings, Sam. Three of the foals that were born this spring look very promising."

"Oi'll 'ave a look at that young 'orse Oi were a-talking to ye about, Miss," Sam said. "The owner's a friend o' mine, and 'e might have others that'd be worth training."

They entered into an animated discussion as to how they could best spend the precious money allotted to them.

Alita knew that she must concentrate on the work she must do in the future, when the excitement of helping Clint Wilbur was no longer there.

'He will build his own race-course,' she thought, 'and then I shall never see him.'

Again the agony she had felt first thing that morning was back. Then she remembered how kind he had been and what fun they had had racing each other over the jumps.

She was up earlier than usual the next morning, and even Sam grumbled because she hurried him when he was getting the horses saddled.

She went off with the two stable-boys, each riding one horse and leading another, while she rode Flamingo and led Rajah.

When she reached the race-course she stared in astonishment.

In the centre of the field, which had been empty yesterday when she had left it, there was now another and very much smaller course with seven jumps.

It only took her a moment to realise that what Clint Wilbur had built was an outdoors replica of the Riding-School.

There was even a small fence round the outside of the jumps so that the horses would feel that they were enclosed as they would be by walls.

She could hardly believe that he could have taken so much trouble on her behalf, and had saved her from disobeying the Duke's orders by bringing to her everything that was essential.

When she saw him appear in the distance she rode towards him impulsively.

Her eyes were shining as she reached him and said:

"How could you have thought of anything so wonderful? Thank you! Thank you a thousand times!"

"I thought it would please you," he answered, "and I also consider it much better for Burt and me to practise in the open air, especially if we have thick heads after too much port the night before!"

Alita knew he was only disparaging his own gen-

The Race for Love

erosity and making it unnecessary for her to go on thanking him.

The horses at first found it a little difficult to take the jumps so quickly one after another.

But Alita soon saw how really outstanding riders like Clint Wilbur and his friend could get their mount off on the right foot to ensure that the horse's balance and timing were perfect.

Rajah made several mistakes on the first time round, which she knew was her fault, but she watched the two men until she could copy them exactly.

As Clint Wilbur had said, when she jumped with Flamingo, he knew what she was thinking and what she wanted of him, because they worked together instinctively.

It seemed to Alita all through the week that the hours on the race-course flew by.

Because she was so anxious not to let Clint Wilbur down, she would often slip back again alone in the afternoon to take Rajah and Flamingo over the jumps patiently and painstakingly until it seemed almost impossible that they could miss a step.

She also every day tried out the new tricks that she was teaching Flamingo, and when she went to bed at night she was so tired that she fell asleep almost before her head touched the pillow.

She had found a book in the Library some time ago which described what the Lipizzaner stallions in the Spanish Riding-School were taught to do when they gave their performance, which was one of the wonders of the horse-loving world.

Flamingo was learning quickly, and although he would never be as magnificent as the famous Lipizzaner stallions, each of which had his own private and ceremonious dance, Alita was certain that he would captivate and entrance any lover of horseflesh.

Barbara Cartland

"One would have thought," the Duchess said sourly at dinner one evening when there were no guests and Alita was therefore allowed to dine with them, "that you might have spent a little of your valuable time helping Hermione and me to prepare for our visit to Windsor."

"I am sorry, Aunt Emily," Alita said quickly, "but I had no idea that you needed me."

"Another pair of hands is often necessary," the Duchess said coldly, "but I quite understand that the horses' needs are more important than my daughter's and mine!"

"I am sorry," Alita said again humbly. "Is there anything I can do for you this evening?"

She knew that when her aunt hesitated, her services were not really needed and that the Duchess, who had been extremely disagreeable towards her recently, was only being deliberately unpleasant.

It was almost as if she had sensed that Alita's eagerness to go to Marshfield House had not been due entirely to the renovation of the stables.

Alita was sure that when her aunt looked at her disparagingly she was thinking that no man would notice her, especially Mr. Wilbur, who had not fallen in love with Hermione; and yet one could never be sure.

It was important from the Duke and Duchess's point of view that no-one, especially a near-neighbour, should have the slightest idea that Alita was closely related to them.

But Alita was quite certain that what her aunt said when she had aroused the Duke to take action was:

"A servant, as Alita is supposed to be, would not be allowed to go gallivanting away from her usual work as your niece has been doing. I do not really approve, Lionel, as you well know, of her working in the stables; but if that is your choice then it is to be in our stables, and, as we decided originally, she is not to leave the environs of the Castle."

After three years of living under her aunt's jurisdiction Alita could be aware of what the Duchess was thinking without her actually speaking the words in her cold, contemptuous manner.

But while in the past she would have been depressed and humiliated by her aunt's attitude, it was impossible at the present to feel anything but an impatience for the moment when they would all leave the Castle for their visit to Windsor.

They actually departed on Friday morning, amidst a flurry of last-minute instructions, forgotten cases, a change of clothing, and a good deal of disagreeableness from the Duke.

He disliked, as Alita knew, travelling with his wife and daughter.

He much preferred going to London alone, and if they were all staying at Langstone House in Park Lane, the Duchess and Hermione would join him later or the next day.

This was the first time that the Duchess had insisted on their travelling together, and Alita was thankful that she did not have to be with them or become involved in the arguments which she was quite certain would keep them bickering the whole way to London.

As the carriage drove away down the drive and she stood on the steps to watch them go, she felt as if the sun came out and a weight fell from her shoulders.

She was free! Free for the rest of the day and for the whole of Saturday and Sunday and part of Monday!

It was almost too good to realise, and she was singing as she ran upstairs to change from her brown gown into her riding-habit.

She was not really surprised that while she was

taking Flamingo over the jumps on the new miniature race-course Clint Wilbur should join her.

He was smiling as he rode across the field and when he reached her he asked:

"They have gone?"

"Yes!"

It seemed disloyal but irrepressible that her voice should ring out with a lilt in it.

Although she was not aware of it, it was not only what she said but the way she looked which told Clint Wilbur of her relief and her excitement.

"Now we have to get busy!" he said.

She waited and he went on:

"I suggest you bring Flamingo to the Riding-School right away. He has to get used to the lights and of course to the music."

"I had not thought of that!" Alita exclaimed.

"They will affect him more than the others, so we will rehearse them tomorrow."

"Yes, of course."

"What I suggest," he went on, "is that you inform your Head-groom that I require delivery of the horses which are going to perform at the Riding-School first thing tomorrow morning."

"I will tell Sam," Alita answered.

She thought that the stables would have been ready by now, but she understood that Clint Wilbur had deliberately left the horses at the Castle simply so that she could go on training them but without disobeying the Duke's instructions not to go to Marshfield House.

"That will leave only Flamingo for you to ride," Clint Wilbur went on, "and let me say here and now that I shall want you every moment tomorrow for what will really be our dress-rehearsal."

When Alita went into the Riding-School she had been astonished by the changes and what had been done in so short a time.

Only Clint Wilbur, she thought, with his drive and also a complete disregard for expense, could have achieved so much so quickly.

The walls had been painted, the floor was covered in sand, all the seats had been removed, and in the balcony new ones covered in a rich crimson velvet looked both comfortable and luxurious.

There were red velvet curtains to draw over the high windows and a special place had been made for the musicians at the end of the Gallery.

Where obviously the Guests of Honour were to sit, flowers were being banked as if Royalty was to be present.

As she looked at it Alita thought to herself that that was true in a way, because Nellie Farren was undoubtedly the Queen of her profession and certainly Queen of the Gaiety.

While she was staring about, the gas-lights were lit.

They made the Riding-School glow with a magical radiance that had not been there before. Alita saw they had been cleverly arranged so as not to dazzle the horses but to bring out the shine on their coats and doubtless also give a glamour to their riders.

"Well, any criticisms?" Clint Wilbur asked.

"How could there be?" Alita replied. "It is perfect. Just what a Riding-School should be!"

"Take Flamingo around and see if he approves," Clint Wilbur suggested. "I cannot provide him with a full orchestra at the moment, but I will play the piano and see if he appreciates my musical efforts."

He walked up to the Gallery and Alita waited outside the big double-door until she heard the first strains of a Viennese waltz.

She rode Flamingo into the School and took him slowly and gently over the jumps.

He never faltered, and when he completed the course twice she realised that the music had stopped and Clint Wilbur was leaning over the balcony, looking at her.

"It is wonderful!" she exclaimed. "And Flamingo thinks so too!"

"Perhaps he can express himself a little more eloquently, Clint Wilbur suggested.

Alita flashed him a smile to show that she understood what he meant, then she made Flamingo bow his head and then go down on one knee, as she had taught him to do.

Clint Wilbur clapped his hands. Then he said:

"You have made a list, as I asked you to do, of the music which is required for Flamingo's solo performance?"

"I have it here in my pocket," Alita answered.

"I have told the leader of the orchestra to be prepared for it," Clint Wilbur said, "so if you give it to me I will leave it on his stand."

Alita drew it out and held it up.

By leaning far over the balcony and stretching down, Clint Wilbur could take it from her.

As he did so their fingers touched and once again she felt the strange sensation that had run through her when he had touched her hand in the Library.

Her eyes were up-turned and as they looked into his blue ones it seemed as if they spoke to each other, and yet what they said could never be expressed in words.

Then with an effort Alita rode Flamingo through the double-doors and brought him in again so that he could grow used to the change of light.

All three of them worked all day Saturday at what Clint Wilbur called the "dress rehearsal," although they wore their ordinary clothes.

For the first time Alita saw the amazing tricks that Burt Ackberg could do.

He could ride twirling a rope round his head, and he could imitate the Cossacks by taking jumps while standing up on the saddle without falling off.

"You ought to be in a Circus!" Alita said, laughing as she clapped her hands at his amazing achievements.

"I have been!" he replied.

When she looked surprised, Clint Wilbur told her:

"He owned it and he gave the money which his performances brought in, which was quite a considerable sum, to a Hospital for sick children."

Alita found that the company of the two men, who teased her and made her laugh and listened to anything she had to say, made her feel she had never been so happy.

Clint Wilbur insisted that they stop work to eat a large luncheon, and again for tea.

When Burt Ackberg protested, he said solemnly:

"You are in England now. Miss Blair, being English, could not possibly carry on without the customary cup of tea."

"Customary is the right word!" Burt Ackberg exclaimed. "They've got some mighty strange customs in England. But if the hunting is as good as I'm told it'll be, I'll put up with having to wear a stiff shirt and a tail-coat for dinner and holding my knife and fork like my grandma's knitting-needles!"

"There are many worse things than that!" Clint Wilbur warned him.

"I know. I'm learning every day, but if you tell me again that my clothes are wrong, I swear I'll go back to Texas tomorrow morning!"

Both Clint Wilbur and Alita cried out that they could not give the performance without him.

She found herself laughing helplessly when he parodied the English way of talking and demonstrated what he considered the "snooty-nosed manner" of shaking hands.

Barbara Cartland

It was all such fun that when, as the sun was sinking, Alita rode back towards the Castle she told herself that if there had not been another exciting day ahead of her she would have felt like crying.

The two men escorted her as far as the wood, and when she was on the Duke's land they raised their hats and she rode on alone.

She knew that Clint Wilbur was safe-guarding her reputation even from the servants at the Castle.

Later in the evening she could not help thinking a little wistfully of the jokes they would be exchanging as they dined at Marshfield House while she was alone in the quiet and gloom of the Castle.

She fell asleep thinking that tomorrow would not come soon enough, but she knew it was here now.

For the first time she wondered how much Clint Wilbur was enjoying himself with his guests.

They would have arrived the night before, and he had told her a little about the preparations he had made for their visit.

First of all—it seemed incredible—he had hired a special train to bring them from London to the nearest railway station to Marshfield House after the performance at the Gaiety was over.

Alita had never been on a private train but her father had told her how comfortable they were.

The special train in which the Prince of Wales travelled on his visits to the country was, he had said, decorated like a comfortable house.

Servants in livery waited on the guests, even providing a seven- or eight-course dinner exactly as if they had been in their own home.

'There will be flowers and champagne,' Alita thought to herself.

But who could deserve it more than Nellie Farren?

There was no need for Clint Wilbur to tell her

that "little Nellie" had been the idol of London for years. But while Nellie Farren was one thing, Miss Wadman was certainly another.

It was she who was Clint Wilbur's special friend, and over and over again Alita found herself repeating in her mind what she had read about Miss Wadman.

She thought there had been a warmth in Clint Wilbur's voice when he spoke of her, and now, riding towards Marshfield House, she told herself that perhaps he was in love with his countrywoman.

Why else would he have made such very extensive preparations for her visit? Why else a performance in the Riding-School which would obviously intrigue and flatter her?

The idea was a pain that was worse than anything Alita had felt before, worse even than the thought of the loneliness to come when everything was over.

'He would be bound to love someone like that,' Alita thought, 'beautiful, and of course vivacious.'

It was not surprising that someone as intelligent and indeed as brilliant as Clint Wilbur would find Englishwomen dull.

'How little I know,' Alita thought, 'and Hermione, although she is beautiful, is ignorant on almost every subject in which Clint Wilbur is interested.'

She thought of how well he played the piano and wondered if Miss Wadman ever sang for him in the voice that had been extolled by the critics.

He would like that, she was sure, and she wondered suddenly if it was too late for her to turn back and not go through with the performance which lay ahead of her.

Then she told herself that to do such a thing would be insulting rather than disappointing to a man who had shown her nothing but kindness.

"At least," Alita told herself almost defiantly, "I

have been with him, I have talked to him, we have laughed together, and there has been no-one else there."

She reached the stables at Marshfield House and carried out the instructions that had been given to her in detail by Clint Wilbur.

She left Flamingo with the grooms and went into the house by a side-door which opened onto the staircase that led her directly up to the first floor.

"I do not want anyone to see you until the curtain goes up," Clint Wilbur had said. "Go to the bedroom you have used before. Everything will be waiting for you."

Alita obeyed him and when she walked into the room she saw at first glance that her two habits, one black and the other grey, were lying on the bed.

Waiting for her was a middle-aged woman.

"Good-evening!" Alita said.

"Good-evening, Miss," the woman replied. "I'm Miss Farren's dresser."

Alita looked at her in astonishment and she went on:

"Mr. Wilbur has asked that I arrange your hair for you and help you into your clothes."

"That is very kind," Alita said, "but I do not like to put you to any trouble."

"It's no trouble, Miss, and Miss Nellie Farren was only too pleased to agree, when Mr. Wilbur suggested it, that I should make you look the part, so to speak!"

She laughed at her own joke and said:

"You get undressed, Miss. I've a wrap here for you to wear while I sees to your hair."

She held out a delectable silk wrap trimmed with lace, but Alita was too shy to ask if it belonged to Nellie Farren.

Instead she quickly took off her old habit, and her petticoats, which had been patched a dozen times, then put on the robe and sat down at the dressing-table.

Because she wanted to look her best she had washed her hair first thing that morning and used, as the Milliner had suggested, the yolks of eggs as a rinse.

When it fell over her shoulders the dresser said as she picked up a brush:

"You've got very pretty hair, Miss. I see you've washed it today."

"I am afraid it may make it difficult to handle," Alita said apologetically.

"I can handle any sort of hair," the dresser replied with a smile. "Miss Farren's hair is soft and sometimes difficult to get into shape, but then she's so frequently playing a boy's part that she prefers to have it cut short, as it'll be in our new Show: *Little Jack Sheppard.*"

"I hope it will be a big success," Alita said.

"Oh, it will be, with Miss Farren in the lead!" the dresser replied.

"I have always longed to see her."

"And she's anxious to see you, hearing what Mr. Wilbur's been telling her."

"I can hardly believe that!" Alita answered. "My father used to tell me about the huge crowds waiting outside the stage-door to see her leave at night just because everybody had loved her performance!"

She smiled.

"My father once said that Nellie Farren was like an electric spark."

"That's true enough, Miss," the dresser agreed, "but how she maintains her tremendous vitality has always been a mystery to me. She hardly eats anything but bread and butter. I suppose the fact is, she lives on her nerves."

She gave a laugh and added:

"The applause of her public is a tonic to her, and that's a fact!"

As she went on brushing Alita's hair in a manner which seemed almost to make sparks fly from it, she continued talking.

She told Alita how Nellie Farren's public took care of her.

"She has to pass through some rough parts on her way home, so a party of men has formed a bodyguard for her, and every evening after the performance they run beside her carriage."

"How wonderful!" Alita exclaimed. "Does she know them?"

"Oh, no, Miss. They're just her admirers, and when they've escorted her carriage through the bad streets they just fade away."

"It is the most flattering thing I have ever heard!" Alita exclaimed.

"They don't ask for thanks," the dresser went on, "but it's people like that as fills the Gallery night after night."

The dresser was still talking as she waved Alita's hair with curlers like those she had seen her mother use.

They were heated over a small burner filled with mentholated spirits. Then the dresser swept Alita's long hair round her head somewhat in the manner worn by the Princess of Wales.

It not only made her look quite different, but there were no wisps or ends to fall untidily round her cheeks and neck as there had always been in the past.

Then, almost before she realised what was happening, the dresser had taken out a pair of scissors and cut her a small, fashionable fringe.

It softened her face and also seemed in some strange way to make her eyes look bigger and more expressive than they had ever appeared before.

"I do not look like myself any longer," Alita said almost to herself.

The Race for Love

"Wait till you get your new habit on and your hat," the dresser said, "then you'll see a difference! It's the black one first, Mr. Wilbur said."

The Empress of Austria might have been sewn into her habit, but Alita thought that nothing could fit tighter or more perfectly than the one which the tailor had made for her.

She had never realised before that she had such a tiny waist, and the perfect figure the bodice-habit gave her would, she knew, be accentuated even more when she was riding a horse.

The top-hat was set at exactly the right angle on her exquisitely dressed hair and was, with its gauze veil falling behind her head, very becoming.

She looked at herself in astonishment, feeling that no-one, and certainly not her uncle or her aunt, would recognise her at this moment.

The dresser looked at the clock on the mantelpiece.

"If we were in the Theatre," she said with a smile, "there would be someone knocking on the door now to say: 'Time, please, Miss Blair!'"

"I must go downstairs," Alita said quickly. "And thank you! Thank you!"

She picked up her new riding-gloves, which had been laid on the bed beside her habit, and a whip she had never seen before with a silver handle.

Then, in her new boots, which she thought made her feet look tiny, she hurried down the passage.

Clint Wilbur had agreed that they should meet in the stables and mount their horses outside the big doors that opened into the Riding-School.

When she saw him waiting for her beside Rajah she suddenly felt shy.

She saw his eyes flicker over her as if appraising her appearance, then he looked directly at her face.

As if he realised that she felt embarrased by his scrutiny, he said with a smile:

"Rajah will be proud of you!"

A stable-boy held Rajah while Clint Wilbur lifted her onto the saddle.

As he arranged her skirt over the brightly polished toe of her boot in what she saw was a silver stirrup, she guessed that it was because Rajah was a black stallion that Clint Wilbur had ordered the first habit she wore to be black too.

She knew that even in the hunting-field with the smart Society ladies who rode with the Quexby she would be outstanding.

But she could not help feeling that it was a little sad that this should be a one-night performance only, and that no-one would ever see her looking like this again.

Then she told herself that it was not a moment for regrets but for enjoyment, even though she was nervous of what lay ahead.

As if he knew that she felt butterflies dancing in her stomach, Clint Wilbur put his hand on hers.

"You will be sensational, as you always are!" he said. "Burt will break in the ice by making them laugh."

Even as he spoke, Alita heard a great roar of laughter coming from the Riding-School.

She realised that she had been so intent on looking at and listening to Clint Wilbur that she had not noticed that there was music in the background and the performance had begun.

She was tense, and yet at the same time she was confident that however frightened she might be, Rajah would not let her down as she rode in through the big double-doors.

For a moment she could see nothing but a glow of golden light and the first fence ahead.

Then gradually, as Rajah took his jumps one after another without a fault, she became aware that there was a larger number of people than she had expected behind the bank of flowers on the balcony.

Only when she had finished two rounds and took Rajah into the centre to salute those sitting above her did she have a quick glimpse of an attractive, piquant face with eyes as blue as the sea and an enticing red-lipped smile.

Nellie Farren was clapping ecstatically with both hands, as were a number of gentlemen who were standing or sitting beside several other women in the comfortable velvet seats.

Somehow—and Alita knew it was stupid of her—she had thought that Nellie Farren and Miss Wadman would be Mr. Wilbur's only guests.

She had not anticipated that there would be at least twenty people on the balcony, and the noise of their applause seemed almost deafening as she turned and rode out through the doors at the end of the School.

She passed Clint Wilbur as he was riding in on King Hal, and he said just one word:

"Perfect!"

Then she was outside and King Hal was leaping over the jumps.

She found Burt Ackberg waiting for her and she saw the admiration in his eyes before he remarked in his drawling voice:

"No wonder you laid them in the aisles!"

"They were laughing at you," Alita said. "I wish I could have seen what you were doing."

"Just making a clown of myself," he replied. "It's a habit of mine."

They had never been alone together before, and as they waited side by side for Clint Wilbur to come from the Riding-School, Alita asked curiously:

"Have you known Mr. Wilbur for many years?"

"Almost since we both arrived in this wicked world," Burt Ackberg replied. "You mean he hasn't told you that our ranches are side by side in Texas?—or rather there's only about five miles between them."

"Five miles is considered a long way over here," Alita remarked.

"That's because this is such a small island," he replied. "I could almost put it in my pocket and take it home."

"You are forgetting our far-flung Empire!" Alita retorted.

"We could pack it all into America and there'd be nothing drooping over the sides," he answered.

She laughed, then said:

"Are you going to stay with Mr. Wilbur for long?"

"He wants me to hunt here with him," Burt Ackberg answered, "and it would be a new experience."

Alita thought privately that it would also be a new experience for the members of the Quexby Hunt, but she did not say so.

A moment later Clint Wilbur came from the Riding-School, with the applause of his guests following him like a roar of the sea.

He joined them to say:

"Now for our race. You go first, Burt. Someone is explaining the rules and will start the clock."

This was an enormous clock, which Alita had already seen, which had been erected so that the guests could watch the seconds tick by and know exactly who was in the lead.

It is all so professional, she thought, and as Burt Ackberg rode away she turned her head to say to Clint Wilbur:

"I am beginning to think that you could produce a Show at the Gaiety without any difficulty, although I have always understood that it is a very hard thing to ensure a theatrical success."

"I might try it one day," Clint Wilbur replied. "Are you suggesting yourself for the lead?"

"Oh, no, of course not!" Alita said, laughing. "Who could compete with Nellie Farren?"

"I agree—she is amazing!" Clint Wilbur said. "And she and Miss Wadman will ensure that *Little Jack Sheppard* is a roaring success."

Again Alita felt a pain which she told herself was envy.

Then, before she could say any more, Burt Ackberg's round was finished and it had been planned that she should go next.

Rajah realised what was expected of him and he moved quicker, Alita thought, than he had ever done before in his whole life.

She and Rajah seemed to fly over the fences, and the applause for their performance started even before they took the last fence.

Then as she rode breathlessly through the doors Alita heard Burt Ackberg saying something to her, but she knew that she had no time to stop and hear what it was.

Instead, she slipped down from Rajah's back and ran through the door which led into the house and up the stairs to the bed-room.

Nellie Farren's dresser had obviously been told how little time Alita had in which to change, and therefore the dresser had everything ready.

She seemed to Alita to whisk her habit from her, and then she was wearing the grey one almost before she could count to ten!

She changed her hat and picked up a different pair of gloves, and then once again she was running down the stairs and out into the yard, where Flamingo was waiting for her.

It was when she was in the saddle that she realised, almost as if she were seeing it with a spectator's eyes, how clever Clint Wilbur had been in choosing that particular tone of grey for her habit.

She made an ensemble with Flamingo that was not only theatrically but esthetically perfect.

The audience obviously thought the same thing, for as she entered the Riding-School there was a burst of applause even before she had started to show them what Flamingo could do.

Then as she took him into the centre of the School to make his bow to those sitting in the balcony, she was aware that unseen hands were pulling aside the fences to give her more room for what she had taught Flamingo to do.

The band began to play a waltz from *Der Rosenkavalier* and she took him round slowly in a circle. Then his head lifted, his neck arched, and his forefoot went out in an arrogant, beautiful movement.

He began to dance in the way that Alita had taught him, waltzing, walking, then waltzing again, and then back to the centre to bow, again a little arrogantly, as if he were conscious of his own achievement.

The music changed and now he rose, rearing magnificently and in time to the melody that was being played.

It was part of the "Airs Above Ground," which were the complicated, traditional steps performed by the Lipizzaner horses in the Spanish Riding-School.

They were difficult, but Flamingo's movements were proud, quiet, and soberly controlled, and yet to those who watched them he seemed to be enjoying himself and to understand exactly the intricate pattern his movements made.

When the music came to an end Alita took him once more to the centre, where he bowed, then went down on one knee, his head touching the ground while she remained sitting straight, only raising her whip to her forehead in a proud salute.

Even with so few people watching, it seemed as if they would take the roof off the Riding-School, so enthusiastic was their applause.

Then, because anything else would have been an anti-climax, she rode Flamingo slowly and majestically out into the yard.

Outside, Clint Wilbur lifted her from the saddle.

"You were marvellous! Wonderful!" he said. "Now go and change quickly!"

She felt as if the words were like a dash of cold water in her face.

Change quickly!

That meant that he expected her to leave at once, to put on her old habit and go home!

She had not expected to stay for long, but she had thought that perhaps he might introduce her to Nellie Farren and that she could linger for a little while and hear what they had to say about the Show.

Because she was so disappointed at being brought back to reality from the dream-like world in which she and Flamingo had for a few minutes reigned supreme, she said nothing.

She only turned and walked away in case Clint Wilbur should see the hurt in her eyes.

She walked up the stairs, not running lightly as she had done before, but quickly because he had ordered it.

Now she knew that he wanted to get her away.

He wanted to send her home so that his guests would not see her; not know that she was nothing but an unimportant stable-hand, of no consequence in his rich and crowded life.

She reached the door of the bed-room and the dresser was there waiting for her.

"Was it a success, Miss?" she asked. "But I needn't ask the question. You couldn't have been anything else, looking like you do."

"Yes... it was a success," Alita said in a dull voice. "And now I must... change."

"And quickly, I understand, Miss," the dresser said.

She undid the hooks at the back of the riding-bodice.

"I've got everything ready, Miss," she said, "and they've sent some very pretty underclothes with that lovely gown."

Alita felt that she could not have heard her aright, but now she saw that lying not on the bed but laid over a chair was a gown which she had never seen before.

It shimmered in the lights that had been lit in the bed-room and there was something golden about it which made Alita think of sunlight.

"That is not my gown," she said. "I think there must have been some mistake. I have to put on the habit I came in."

"Oh, no, Miss! Those are my instructions," the dresser said.

Alita stared at her wide-eyed.

"Wh-what were your ... instructions?" she asked in a voice that did not sound like her own.

"Mr. Wilbur said you were to change into that dinner-gown, Miss, and there'd be someone waiting to escort you to the Salon."

Chapter Six

One of the guests rose to her feet with obvious reluctance.

"I suppose we ought to go," she said, "but I cannot remember when I have enjoyed an evening more."

It was a sentiment which, Alita knew, everyone in the room could echo with all sincerity.

She herself had found that every moment of the dinner-party and what had followed was so exciting, so unlike any evening she had ever before known, that she longed for it to go on and on and never end.

After dinner, at which the food had been superlative and the wines chosen with a discriminating taste, they had moved into the large Salon, and there everyone seemed ready to give a performance.

Nellie Farren sang and danced, Miss Wadman not only sang herself but got everyone else singing with her, and several other members of the party had talents they were only too willing to display.

Burt Ackberg, who had been told that he was exempt from doing any more, as he had already performed, insisted on showing them some magic tricks, which kept them all guessing.

Another member of the party who had once been on the stage sang some of the old songs that Alita when she was a child had heard her mother play so beautifully that tears had come to her eyes.

Yet it was impossible not to laugh and keep on laughing when Nellie Farren was there.

Alita had no idea that she was so small, and Clint Wilbur had told her at dinner that she liked to think of herself as quite big and therefore her size was never mentioned in her presence.

He also told Alita that her pet aversion was tight boots and shoes. And her feet were so tiny that Alita could not help feeling that it would be far easier to buy ones that were too big than to get ones that fitted her.

Altogether, it was an evening that was very different from the long and gloomy ones that she had spent at the Castle for so many years.

When she was downstairs she was lectured by her aunt, or if she was up, she sat alone in a fireless room.

At the suggestion that the party should break up, other guests who had some distance to go also made a move.

"I can see that having you here in the County," Alita heard one man say to Clint Wilbur, "is going to make things very enjoyable for all of us!"

"That is true," another chimed in. "You will be a real asset, Wilbur, and the M.F.H. asked me to welcome you to the Quexby Hunt. We will all look forward to seeing you at our Opening Meet."

"I am looking forward to it too," Clint Wilbur replied, "and I hope you will extend an equally generous welcome to my friend Burt Ackberg."

"We certainly will!" several people exclaimed at once. "And if he rides to hounds as well as he did this evening in the Riding-School, we shall all be jealous!"

There was a warmth about the way they spoke,

which Alita knew was their way of giving respect to two men whom they recognised as sportsmen.

Any crime, she thought—except one—would be forgiven to men who rode as well as Clint Wilbur and Burt Ackberg.

After saying good-night to Nellie and Miss Wadman, the guests moved down the Salon towards the door, and Alita said in a low voice to Clint Wilbur:

"I must leave . . . too."

"Wait!" he said. "I will take you home."

She looked up in surprise, ready to say that there was no need for him to escort her, but he moved away, going with his guests to the front door.

"It's been a lovely evening!" Nellie Farren said as she sat down on a sofa.

"You were wonderful!" Alita said.

"And so were you, my dear."

"Thank you for saying so. It is a compliment I will always remember."

"You'll get plenty of those, seeing how well you ride," Nellie Farren replied, smiling.

"Of course you will!" Miss Wadman interposed. "And I envy you. I never was much of a rider. I'm always afraid the horse will run away with me."

Alita looked at her in surprise.

Somehow, because she was Clint Wilbur's friend, Alita was sure that Miss Wadman would be a good rider and accompany him in the Park when he was in London; or perhaps they had ridden together when they were in America.

As if she had asked the question, Miss Wadman went on:

"No, I've no wish to have anything to do with horses except sit behind them in a comfortable carriage."

"Mr. Wilbur is such a brilliant rider," Alita said almost as if she was trying to persuade Miss Wadman to take more interest in him.

"I know that," Miss Wadman replied, "but everyone to his—or her—own sport!"

She laughed as she spoke, and Nellie Farren laughed with her.

The two women looked so attractive as they did so that Alita felt again a stab of envy—or was it jealousy?

She felt that she could never be so amusing or so glamorous, and she could understand why they were the type of women that Clint Wilbur liked.

He came back into the room, with Burt Ackberg behind him, to say to Alita:

"They have gone and there is a carriage waiting for you."

"A carriage?" she queried. "But I thought..."

"If you are thinking of riding home," he interrupted, "let me tell you that Flamingo has for the last few hours been in his own stall at the Castle, doubtless dreaming about his success!"

Because she did not like to argue in front of the others, Alita said good-night to Nellie Farren and Miss Wadman.

Burt Ackberg shook her hand heartily.

"You were magnificent!" he said. "And if I ever run another Circus I will offer you the leading role."

"Thank you," Alita replied with a smile; then she went from the Salon, followed by Clint Wilbur.

As soon as they were outside in the Hall she said:

"Please stay with your guests. It is very kind of you to send me home in your carriage, but I shall be quite all right alone."

"I am taking you back," he said firmly, in the voice which she knew brooked no opposition.

A footman came forward with a fur-trimmed velvet wrap which she had not seen before.

Clint Wilbur took it from him and put it round Alita's shoulders.

Feeling very unlike her usual self, Alita walked

down the steps to find a closed Brougham drawn by two horses, with a coachman and a footman on the box.

Clint Wilbur helped her into it, then sat beside her, and the footman put a rug over their knees.

It was a very comfortable carriage and had a silver candle-lantern which lit the elegant interior with a soft golden glow.

The horses started off and Alita turned to Clint Wilbur to say:

"How can I begin to thank you and to tell you what this evening has ... meant to me?"

"What has it meant?" he asked in his deep voice.

"Something I never ... dreamt would ... happen!" she replied. "And it is something I shall remember ... always ... and think about when ..."

"When what?" he asked.

"When it is not ... possible to ... see you again."

"Are you suggesting that we must say good-bye to each other?" he enquired.

"I ... I am afraid so. ... You see ... sooner or later the Duke is bound to find out that you come to the race-course ... and besides, I expect ... now that you have the horses, you will ... build a course of your own."

"Apart from that possibility, it would be helpful, to say the least of it, if you told me why the Duke should object to our meeting."

Alita turned her face away from him to stare ahead so that he could only see her profile silhouetted against the darkness.

"I know it ... annoys you," she murmured, "but I cannot ... answer your questions."

Because she did not wish him to dwell on the subject of herself, she added quickly:

"Before we arrive at the Castle ... I want to ask you how I can ... return this wonderful gown you so kindly lent me for this evening. Perhaps one of your grooms could fetch it tomorrow?"

Barbara Cartland

"It is a present, like your riding-habits," Clint Wilbur answered.

"A... p-present? But I cannot... you know I cannot accept such... expensive gifts."

"And what do you expect me to do with them?" he asked bluntly.

It seemed that there was no answer, and after a moment Alita said a little incoherently:

"When you said you were... dressing me for the part I was to play... I never imagined... I never thought that I might... keep the clothes."

"You look very lovely in all of them."

She was so surprised at the way he spoke that she turned to look at him, her eyes wide and holding in their depths a gleam of light from the lantern.

"Do I really have to tell you," he asked, "that everyone tonight was acclaiming your beauty as well as your talent?"

"You... you are... teasing me!"

"No, I am telling you the truth. I realised a long time ago that this was how you would look if you were properly dressed."

She was so astonished at what he was saying that she could only stammer:

"How... how did you... know?"

He smiled as he replied:

"If you saw a thoroughbred that had been put out to grass and neglected, whose coat was thick and matted, his mane unbrushed, and who had gone wild, as one might say, would you recognise his breeding?"

Alita thought for a moment, then she said:

"I... hope I... would."

"And I recognised when I first saw you that you could look as you do now—very lovely and very fascinating—even though you persist in being mysterious."

It seemed to Alita that he came a little closer as he spoke.

Yet, because she was almost hypnotised by what he was saying and by a note in his voice that she had never heard before, she could not move away.

She could only sit there staring at him, feeling as if he had lit a light within her that was sweeping away the darkness of insecurity and unhappiness, which was all she had known for so long.

"What... can I... say?" she said. "How can I... tell you what... your kindness means to me?"

"Why try?" he replied. "There are so many better ways of saying what one feels besides words."

His arm went round her as he spoke, he lifted her chin, and his lips came down on hers!

For a moment she was too astonished to move, too astonished even to be sure of what was happening.

Then as she felt his other arm go round her and he drew her closer still, she felt his lips evoke that strange streak of quicksilver which had run through her before when his hand had touched hers.

Now it was more intense, more wonderful, more compelling, and she knew that this was what she had longed for, was what subconsciously she had wanted ever since she had known him.

It was love which had made her count the hours until she could meet him on the race-course each morning.

It was love that had made her jealous of the women whom he had planned to entertain so lavishly.

It was love which made her vibrate to him as if she were an instrument played by a master-hand.

Everything that had been starved and neglected in her seemed to break down before a force so strong, so indomitable, that she could only surrender herself completely to the magic and wonder of it.

She felt as if his lips drew her soul and her mind from her body and made them his.

She knew that her every nerve vibrated to a

strange, ecstatic rapture that carried her into a light so brilliant, so overwhelming, that she was blinded and yet at the same time a part of it.

His lips were demanding, possessive, and dominated her to the point where it was impossible to breathe.

In fact it was impossible to do anything but quiver in his arms, and she knew that if she died at this moment it would be the most perfect thing that could happen.

How could she go on living, she thought wildly, without the closeness of him and with the desolation of being alone again?

Suddenly the horses came to a standstill and she knew that they were back at the Castle. She must leave him, and nothing could ever be the same again.

He drew his arms from her as if he too was reluctant, and she gazed at him, bewildered, at the same time feeling as if her whole body was glowing with a strange, unaccountable warmth.

The footman opened the door and Alita managed to alight.

Only when she was standing on the steps did she realise with a feeling of consternation that the servants must have aroused the night-watchman, for the front door was open.

Slowly she walked towards it, aware that Clint Wilbur moved beside her.

They stepped into the Hall, and old Johnson, who had been the night-watchman for years and who was half-blind, quavered:

"I was a-wondering who it could be, Miss Alita. I didn't know as you were out!"

Alita did not reply.

She only moved a little farther into the Hall, which was lit only by a lantern standing by the padded chair in which old Johnson sat when he was not making his rounds.

She looked up into Clint Wilbur's eyes and tried to speak, but, although her lips moved, no words would come.

He looked down at her for a long moment, and then as if he understood he took her hand in his.

"I will see you tomorrow," he said softly, "but not before noon. I want you to rest, and as there are fewer horses now in the stables there will be no reason for you to rise early."

It was an order, not a request. Then he raised her hand to his lips and kissed it.

"Good-night," he said quietly, and turned to walk back to the carriage.

Only when the horses had moved away, and old Johnson had shut the Castle door and bolted it, did Alita see standing on the floor a leather case and two hat-boxes.

She thought that Johnson was going to speak to her, perhaps to repeat his surprise that she was out so late.

Because she could not find words that could be spoken through lips that had been kissed, she turned and ran up the stairs.

* * *

Alita awoke to know even before she looked at the clock that it was far later in the morning than she usually rose.

She might have been late getting back, but it was even later before finally she got into bed.

Last night she had stood staring at herself in the mirror in the bed-room, wondering if the radiant person she saw reflected there could possibly be the despised, neglected, untidy Alita Lang.

How could she have been transformed, as if by a magician's wand, into someone who looked not only beautiful but as elegant and graceful as any of the women she had met that evening?

Only Clint Wilbur, she thought, could have realised that the very pale yellow of her gown was the perfect complement to her strange hair.

It also seemed to make her skin very white and to reflect a golden light into her grey eyes, which made them look different from the way they had always looked before.

Alita knew that it was not only the gown which had made so much difference, but love.

Love had throbbed within her; but instead of diminishing now that she had left Clint Wilbur, it seemed to increase until she felt as if her whole body had come alive in a way she had never known.

"I love him! I love him!" she told her reflection.

Then with a little cry she turned away from the mirror, knowing that her love was hopeless and that the sooner she faced up to the truth the better.

And yet when finally she got into bed it was difficult to think of anything but his kisses and feel again the sensation like quicksilver that in its intensity had been half-ecstasy, half-pain.

"I love him! I love him!"

It was impossible to do anything but repeat the words over and over again until they seemed to echo back at her in the darkness, and she felt as if her love must reach out to him wherever he might be.

"If only I could have died when he kissed me," she whispered, afraid that when the rapture had gone she would be left only with the agony.

Now in the morning light it was easier to think a little more clearly.

Sooner or later he would have to know the truth, but, while her mind knew that it was inevitable, her whole body screamed out in violent protest:

'Not yet! Not yet! Live in your Fool's Paradise a little longer! Perhaps he will kiss you again!'

"I have to think sanely," Alita said to herself.

The kiss he had given her was what any man would give a woman whom he was taking home alone! A woman who was not Socially important enough to have a Chaperon.

But her heart told her something different.

Could a kiss which had been so wonderful, so ecstatic, so perfect in every way, have meant nothing to him?

She was too ignorant, she told herself, of men and their behaviour to know the answer.

She knew only that he had taken her into a Heaven which she had not even known existed, and had brought a light into the darkness of her misery.

To lose him now completely would be an agony that was beyond words, thoughts, or feelings.

Then she remembered that he had said he would see her this morning, and the fear that she might be late brought her quickly out of bed.

It was in fact, she saw with consternation, half-past-ten, an inconceivably late hour for her to be rising.

As the house-maids were very short-handed at the Castle, they never troubled themselves with her, and therefore no-one had come to find out if she had overslept.

They would have expected that as usual she had called herself and been in the stables by six o'clock.

'He will meet me on the race-course,' Alita thought to herself, 'perhaps for the last time.'

She shied away from the thought that if this was so, it would be due to her being forced to tell him the truth as to why she could not meet him again.

She was quite certain that when her aunt returned this afternoon she would be suspicious about what had happened while she and her daughter had been away.

But, however imaginative the Duchess might be, she would never guess the real truth of what had occurred.

"It was marvellous!" Alita said aloud.

After she had washed, she realised that her old habit was probably in the case which had been in the carriage. She wondered if anyone had brought it upstairs.

She opened her bed-room door and found, surprisingly, that Johnson must have staggered up with the case and the hat-boxes.

They were outside the door, and she brought them into the room.

When she had done so, she looked towards the wardrobe as if to reassure herself that the gown she had worn last night was still there.

The door was open and she could see it in the cupboard like a shaft of sunlight.

'I shall never wear it again,' she thought, 'any more than I shall ever wear the riding-habit.'

That, in a way, was even harder to bear, but how could she ever explain the possession of clothes which had come from the most exclusive tailor in London and, she suspected, the most expensive dressmaker?

She knew now who the strange woman had been who had stood watching her in the bed-room at Marshfield House while the tailor was taking her measurements.

Only Clint Wilbur, she thought, could have thought of a way to make her so happy and make her a present of the gown without a tiresome argument about it.

"It is mine now!" Alita murmured. "And when I look at it I shall always think of him."

She opened the leather case, which was a very smart and expensive one and looked as if it had never been used before.

On top were her two new habits, the grey and the black. Underneath, she found the disreputable, threadbare one that she had worn for so long.

The Race for Love

She took out all three, then hesitated.

Should she wear her own, and face reality, or should she just once more appear looking smart and elegant, with a waist that was even smaller than that of the Empress of Austria?

She had a feeling that if she went to Clint Wilbur tattered and untidy, he might perhaps regret that he had kissed her.

Who would want to kiss a scarecrow, which was how she looked ordinarily?

She went to the mirror on the dressing-table to stare at her hair.

Last night when she had gone to bed she had not loosened it as she would normally have done.

She had thought about it and decided that when she took out the pins she would do so very carefully so that she could try to copy the way the dresser had arranged her hair.

To her delight, the pins combined with the way her hair had been waved had survived a night's sleep.

It was only a question of puffing out the sides, which had become a little flattened, putting the hair-pins in a little more securely, and combing the fringe.

There was no need to worry any further about what she should wear. Alita put on the grey habit, fastening it with some difficulty but nevertheless managing it alone.

Then she slipped her feet into the long, elegant, polished boots.

Never had she thought to own anything that was so becoming to her.

She drew her new gloves from the leather case and as she did so she told herself that this was the last time she would ever wear any of these things.

They would have to be hidden away like faded love-letters and kept under lock and key.

She knelt down on the floor to open the hat-boxes, and as she did so there came a knock on the door.

"Who is it?" she asked apprehensively.

"'Tis me, Miss Alita," Barnes replied. "Mr. Wilbur's here to see you, and I've put him in the Drawing-Room." For a moment it was hard to reply, because Alita's heart began to beat suffocatingly.

Then with an effort she managed to answer:

"I ... I will be down in a ... moment, Barnes."

"Very good, Miss."

Why had he come? Alita wondered. Why had he not met her, as she had expected him to do, on the race-course?

She knew that old Barnes would not tell her uncle if she asked him not to. At the same time, she felt that it was somehow ignominious to intrigue with the servants.

Then another thought struck her:

Perhaps something had gone wrong!

But she did not know what it could possibly be. At the same time, it seemed strange that Clint Wilbur should come to the Castle when he was well aware that the Duke would not approve of it.

She pushed the leather case under the bed so that anyone coming into her bed-room would not see it, then hid the hat-boxes in the bottom of the wardrobe, shut the door, and locked it.

Hastily, because she had no wish to keep him waiting, she ran down the stairs.

Clint Wilbur was in the rather austere Drawing-Room, standing in front of the fireplace, in which there was no fire.

He was not wearing riding-clothes, and as Alita walked towards him it flashed through her mind that there had been a misunderstanding.

She had thought that when he had said he would see her at noon, he had meant it be at the race-course.

Then, as she drew nearer, her eyes met his and it was difficult to think of anything but him.

Love welled up inside her so that her heart seemed to pound in her breast like a drum and it was difficult to breathe.

She moved automatically within a few feet of him, and he watched her come.

They stood facing each other without moving. Then he said:

"You are well?"

"Of ... course."

The words they were speaking did not really matter. Something magnetic, like a spark of fire, ran between them.

"Wh ... why have you come ... here?"

Her voice was barely above a whisper.

"I could not wait any longer! I had to see you!"

She drew in her breath at the note in his voice.

"Why?"

He smiled, and it seemed to illuminate his whole face.

"I thought you might guess the answer to that."

She was silent for a moment before she said:

"I ... I was going to ... m-meet you on the race-course."

"I know that," he said, "but I felt that the race-course was not the right place for me to say what I have to say."

She looked puzzled.

"Wh-what ... is that?"

He took a step forward and put his arms round her. As his lips sought hers she seemed to melt against him, and then he was kissing her as he had done last night in the carriage.

Now as he held her even closer and her whole body was touching his, they were no longer two people but one, and she was a part of him.

He kissed her until it seemed that the walls of the Drawing-Room swung round her, until she heard music in her ears and felt as if he carried her into the sunshine and up to a special Heaven that she had never known before.

When finally he raised his head, she could only look at him and say what was in her heart:

"I love ... you!"

She was not even certain if she had said it aloud, but only what the music in her whole body expressed: a love so overwhelming that there was nothing else and no-one else but him in the whole world.

"And I love you, my darling!" he said against her lips. "And what I have come to ask you, is how soon will you marry me?"

For a moment she could hardly believe what she had heard. She just thought it must be part of the glory in her heart.

"I cannot wait," Clint Wilbur went on. "I want you now—immediately—and without any arguments."

It was then that Alita came back to sanity.

With an almost superhuman effort she struggled from his arms; and then, because he was no longer supporting her, she felt that she would fall, so she reached out to hold on to the back of a chair.

"Did you ... ask me to ... marry you?" she questioned in a voice which he could barely hear.

"I said I want you now—at once," he repeated.

She gave a little cry which was almost like that of a small animal that was being hurt.

"It is impossible! Quite ... impossible!"

"Why do you say that?"

"B-because I ... cannot marry you."

"But you love me?"

"Yes ... I love you ... but that has ... nothing to do with it."

"I should have thought it had everything to do with it."

The Race for Love

"No ... no ... you do not .. understand."

"How can I, if you will not tell me why you are refusing me?"

She could not look at him, and he took a step forward to put both his hands on her shoulders.

"What are you hiding?" he asked. "What is this momentous secret that you have hinted at ever since I have know you? Are you already married?"

"No, no! Of course ... not!"

"And you love me?"

"You ... know I ... do!"

"Then we will be married. I have already made all the arrangements."

"How ... could you do ... that?"

"I knew last night that you loved me. I knew too that you would be difficult, as you are being now. But I do not intend to allow anything to stand in the way of my marrying the only woman I have ever wanted as my wife."

For the first time since he had taken hold of her, she raised her eyes to his.

"Is that ... true?" she asked in a wondering tone.

"It is true," he replied. "I have loved you, my darling, ever since you fainted and I carried you to the sofa in the Library. I knew then that I had to look after you and protect you, if necessary from yourself."

She gave a little sigh that was somehow heart-rending.

"If you only ... knew what it ... means to me to hear you ... speak like ... that," she said. "I love you ... so much that I can see or hear nothing except you ... but I cannot ... marry you."

"Why not?"

She thought that he was going to take her in his arms again, and with a strength which she did not know she possessed she moved away from him.

"I will ... tell you what you ... want to ... know," she said; "then you will ... not only understand ...

but you will no... longer wish to... marry me."

Her voice quivered on the words, and he said:

"I cannot imagine anything which would prevent me from loving you as I do now, or which would prevent me from making you my wife if you are free, as you say you are."

His words, spoken in the forceful and determined tone which she knew he always used when he was fighting for what he wanted, brought her to a standstill.

She clasped her hands together and stood looking at him.

He thought he had never seen a woman's eyes hold so much love, and yet at the same time her expression was so tragic, so heart-breaking, that it moved him as nothing in his life had ever done before.

"My darling, what have you done that could make you look like that?" he asked very gently. "If you have committed murder, I will shelter you; if you have committed every other crime in the calendar, we will forget them together."

She tried to smile but failed, and tears fell from her eyes and ran down her cheeks.

"Before I... tell you," she whispered, "and you leave me... will you please... kiss me... once more?"

He held out his arms and she ran towards him.

He pulled her against him, holding her so tightly that it was difficult to breathe.

"Do you really think I would leave you?" he asked.

"You... will," she answered. "I know... that. Kiss me... please kiss me... so that when you are gone ... I can forget... everything except that you... once said you... loved me."

"I shall always love you," he said. "Do not speak of it as if it is something that is past. You are mine, Alita, mine because our love is bigger than anything else in the world—bigger than the crime or whatever secret you are trying to hide."

She did not move or speak, but he knew that she did not believe him.

Despite his resolution and determination, which never before had broken, he began to feel afraid.

"I love you!" he said harshly. "Does that mean nothing to you?"

"It means ... everything ... everything!" she answered. "I thought when I first met you that I would never know love except what I gave the horses and the affection they gave me."

She gave a little sob as she went on:

"And when I first loved you ... it was like looking at the ... moon and knowing that it was far, far away, and quite impersonal. Still, I ... loved you."

"And now?"

"I ... adore and ... worship you," she answered, "and that is ... why I am ... going to ... ask you ... something."

"What is it?"

"When I have ... told you what you ... want to .. hear ... will you please go away without saying ... anything? Just ... leave ... for I could not ... bear your ... pity."

Tears were running down her face but her eyes still looked up into his.

Then as her voice broke on the last words, his lips were upon hers.

He kissed her passionately, fiercely, possessively, in a very different manner from the way he had before.

She knew that he was fighting her with kisses, battling with a love that was demanding and dominating and violent.

It made her love him desperately, frantically, and she wanted only to surrender herself to everything he asked of her and to be his completely and absolutely.

'Oh, God, let me die!' she prayed silently.

At the same time, something wild and wonderful responded to the fire in him and she wanted to live.

While he kissed her it seemed as though time stood still.

Then, as if they both knew that the moment had come when the truth must be spoken, she moved from the shelter of his arms and he did not try to stop her.

She walked to the window. Although the sun was shining she thought it was a grey day, and the gardens seemed to her shrouded in darkness.

She knew he was waiting, but for a long time the words would not come to her lips and she felt as if she had suddenly been stricken with a paralysis so that even her brain had ceased to function.

Then at last, in a trembling voice, she said:

"The ... D-Duke is my ... uncle!"

"Your uncle?"

She knew by the surprise in Clint Wilbur's voice that this was something he had not expected to hear.

"My father was his ... younger brother, Lord Edward Lang," Alita went on, "and he was a very ... different character in every way. He loved ... gaiety and all the ... good things of life that were ... denied him."

"Why were they denied to him?"

"Because he was the second son, and, as is usual in England, the eldest son inherited everything. My father had only a very small allowance when he was a young man, and after he married my mother he was always ... hard-up and found it ... difficult to make ... ends meet."

"And the Duke did not help him?"

"The Duke himself is very short of money, as you must be aware."

Clint Wilbur did not speak, and Alita went on, still with her back towards him:

"As the years went by, my father got... deeply into... debt. Then my mother became ill. The Doctors told him that if she was to... live, she must have an... expensive operation."

"Surely the Duke..." Clint Wilbur began.

"My father was just going to ask his brother to help him over my mother's illness, when something... unforeseen and very... terrible happened."

"What was that?"

"He had helped a friend who was in... temporary difficulties... by backing a cheque for several thousand... pounds."

Alita paused for a moment, then went on:

"It was only a question of waiting a week or so for the money to arrive from his friend's father. If he had not been able to pay his gambling-debts... which as you know are debts of honour... it would have been very... unpleasant for him."

"I understand—so he disappeared!"

"No... no! He would... never have done that... but he was... killed out... hunting."

There was silence as Alita paused, and then Clint Wilbur said:

"So your father was faced with having to find the money?"

"He was desperate... absolutely desperate... and he knew it would be almost impossible for Uncle Lionel, even if he had been willing... to find such a large sum."

There was another silence, and after a while Clint Wilbur asked:

"What did he do?"

It was as if Alita could not bring herself to say the words. Then at last, almost in a whisper, they came from her lips:

"He... had had... a great deal to... drink, and

he went to his... Club in... St. James's, and... and he..."

Again there was a silence before she went on in a hurried little voice, as if she must say the words as quickly as possible:

"He... cheated at... cards! He was... seen doing it not only by his... friends but also by several... acquaintances."

She gave a pitiable little sob.

"There was no... question of being able to... hush it up. Papa knew too that it would bring... disgrace not only on... us but on the whole... family!"

Again there was silence; then Alita said in a voice which Clint Wilbur could barely hear:

"He... he shot himself... he felt that it was the only... honourable thing he... could do."

As she spoke, she bowed her head and put her hands up to her face.

She had said it; now he knew what had happened.

It was impossible to put into words the horror of what had followed. Her uncle's anger, her mother's death a month later, and the decision that she must disappear so that the whole episode would gradually be forgotten.

"No-one would ever ask you inside their houses," the Duke had said harshly. "No-one would associate with the daughter of a cheat. You cannot even work for your living, because it would be impossible for anyone to give you a reference."

He paused before saying sharply and contemptuously:

"I will take you to the Castle, but you must quite understand that you will not meet my friends; and no-one, except the servants who have known you since you were a child, must even be aware that I have a niece."

His voice had been bitter as he had added:

"I am ashamed, deeply ashamed, that any brother of mine should have behaved in such a way. But he is dead, your mother is dead, and as far as the rest of the world is concerned you are dead too!"

The way he had spoken made Alita feel as if she were already buried.

For a long time she had crept about the Castle, feeling that she was only a ghost of her former self and being surprised when people actually saw that she was there.

Then she had worked with the horses and made some kind of life for herself.

The Duchess had always despised her, and she knew that nine times out of ten when her uncle looked at her he saw a blot on the family name and hated her as he hated the memory of his own brother.

She felt tears trickling through her fingers but still there was not the sound she expected. She listened to hear Clint Wilbur leaving, opening the door and walking out of her life.

She felt the agony of it like a thousand daggers in her breast.

Then suddenly he spoke, and she knew that he had not moved.

"Is that—all?"

There was in his voice a note which she did not understand, and she could not answer, thinking that there was no reply she could give to his question, and her tears began to fall even faster.

Now she wanted him to leave, wanted him to go, wanted the agony to be over so that she could collapse completely.

Then suddenly his arms were round her and he was holding her close against him.

"My darling, my sweet!" he said, and she thought she could not be hearing aright. "Why did you not tell me all this before? Did you think it would matter to me?"

"B-but...he...cheated!" she managed to stammer, thinking that perhaps he had not understood. "Papa... cheated at cards!"

"My father is always supposed to have cheated to gain an entire railroad," Clint Wilbur answered, "and my grandfather definitely cheated his partner out of a gold-mine!"

There was a note of amusement in his voice, and now as he pulled Alita's hands away from her face, she saw, to her utter astonishment, that he was smiling.

"Do you really think, my absurd, ridiculous darling, that a few cards, however manipulated by your father, could keep me from making you my wife?"

She stared up at him, thinking that she could not have heard him correctly, but he went on:

"I am prepared to cheat in every Club, to pull my horses on every race-course, and certainly to cheat your uncle, if that is the only way I can have you!"

He paused for a moment, then added:

"And the latter is exactly what I intend to do!"

Then he was kissing her again, so it was quite impossible for Alita to answer him.

Chapter Seven

Clint raised his head and, with a smile on his lips, looked down at Alita's flushed, excited face.

"Go upstairs, my lovely one," he said. "Collect the gown you wore last night and your other habit. You will not need anything else."

"But...I...do not...understand," Alita managed to say.

She was shy from the wild excitement of his kisses, and being so close in his arms had aroused emotions she had never known before.

"We are to be married," he said. "Have you forgotten?"

"Now?" she enquired.

"In a few hours," he replied, "and the sooner we are on our way, the better!"

"But...how can...we...how can we...leave without...telling...Uncle Lionel?"

"I will do that," Clint said grimly. "I will leave him a note, which is all he deserves for the way he has treated you."

"He always said that...no man would ever marry me."

"Except me," Clint said with a smile, "and I am glad—very glad—that I have no rivals."

He put his hand under her chin and turned her face up to his.

"Do you realise how beautiful you are?" he said. "I shall be a very jealous husband!"

"How could you think... how could you... imagine that I would ever... look at anyone... except you?" she asked. "I love you so... overwhelmingly that it is impossible to know that there are any other... men in the whole world."

The touch of passion in her voice moved him and he laid his cheek against hers.

"I love you too," he said, "and there will be plenty of time for us to tell each other of our love, but now I am anxious to be on our way. The train is waiting."

"The... train?" Alita questioned. "But... where are we... going?"

"To be married," he answered, "and that will take place on our way to Holyhead."

She stared at him in wonder, and he explained:

"We are going to Ireland. I think it would be a new experience for both of us to hunt there this winter. And when we get back to Marshfield you will be my wife, and I shall defy anyone not to accept you as warmheartedly as they accept me."

"But... Uncle Lionel?" Alita said, faltering.

"What the Duke does or does not do is of very little consequence," Clint Wilbur answered. "But I have a feeling that he will be wise enough to be gracious to his neighbour's wife."

Alita thought that this was likely. The Duke would be conscious of the financial benefits he would gain in having such a rich neighbour; and once he had got over the shock, he would find some explanation for their relationship.

But she told herself that nothing mattered except that she would be with her husband.

"But how... can you leave the... horses?" she asked.

She knew that he would have an answer, but because it all seemed so incredible, so amazing, she had to ask for an explanation.

"They will be in safe hands," he answered, "including Flamingo."

He knew that she was waiting, and he added:

"Burt has promised to stay and look after them, and he will hunt with the Quexby until we return."

"You have thought of... everything," Alita said with a little sigh. "But I am still... afraid."

"Of me?"

"No, of course not! Of running... away. I know Uncle Lionel will be very... angry."

"He will recover," Clint said with a sarcastic little twist of his lips. "And I do not intend you to be upset or involved in any arguments. You know how much I dislike them."

She pressed herself a little closer to him.

"I am not arguing," she said, "but... how can I be... married in a... riding-habit?"

"You look very lovely in it," he replied. "But actually you will find a very suitable gown, and a number of other things you will require, waiting for you in the train."

She gave a little cry.

"How could you have done anything so... fantastic? How could you be so... marvellous... to... me?"

Her voice broke and she hid her face so that he could not see her tears.

This could not be happening. This could not be real!

After three years of being despised, ignored, and snubbed, that Clint should love her and want to marry her was almost too much to bear.

As if he understood what she was feeling, he said very gently:

"It is all in the past, and the future, my darling, is ours."

He knew that she made an effort at self-control, and he took a handkerchief from his pocket and wiped away her tears.

It was of very soft linen and smelt of eau-de-cologne, and because he was so gentle it made her want to cry all the more.

"Hurry upstairs," he said. "There is so much to talk about, so much to tell each other, and if you do not go now we shall be standing here like statues when your uncle and aunt return."

If anything could have made Alita move quickly it was the thought of encountering the Duke and his anger, or hearing the Duchess's sharp voice reprimanding her.

She knew that even while Clint would defend her, it would spoil the dream-like quality which now enveloped her like a rainbow.

It was all so perfect, so like the happy ending of a fairy-story, that she knew it must not be touched by rough fingers or spoilt by quarrels and recriminations.

"I will go," she said.

Then because she loved him so overwhelmingly, she pressed her lips to his cheek.

He pulled her almost violently against him, and the fire was back in his eyes; but, as if he thought it was a mistake to delay things any further, he merely kissed her swiftly and said:

"I give you five minutes and not a second longer! Where can I write a note to your uncle?"

"There is a writing-table in the Library next door," Alita said.

Then, thinking how much there was to do in only five minutes, she ran across the Hall and upstairs to her bed-room.

No-one had been there since she had left, and she pulled the leather case out from under the bed. Throwing aside her old habit and her disreputable old boots, she repacked the black habit she had worn last night and on top of it she laid the beautiful yellow evening-gown with its lace-trimmed petticoats. There were masses of tissue paper to keep it from being creased.

Having closed the case, she then fetched the hat-boxes from the locked wardrobe.

One, she thought, would travel empty because she must wear the grey hat which matched her habit.

She put it on in front of the mirror and found it hard to recognise herself in the starry-eyed reflection that looked back at her.

Could this really be the same girl who when she dressed in the morning had never looked in a mirror because there would be no-one to see her except the horses?

No-one to care if she was tidy or untidy, ugly or pretty.

A paean of gratitude rose within her as she thought how her life had changed.

"Thank you, God! Thank you, God!" she cried.

Because she felt that her father, wherever he was, would know that she would no longer suffer because of him, she sent a little prayer winging towards him.

"I understand, Papa," she told him, "why you behaved as you did, but now the nightmare is over and I have found love ... the love of a man who is not ... shocked, as all the other people have been."

Then as she turned from the mirror she was still a little doubtful.

Supposing Clint was just being kind? Supposing really he minded deep down inside that his wife should be the daughter of a man who had been ostracised by all his friends?

Barbara Cartland

She had lived so long with the belief that a gentleman who cheated at cards could never again raise up his head, that the shame was still there.

Supposing, just supposing...

She thought that perhaps Clint had not fully understood what she had told him!

Picking up her case with one hand, and managing with difficulty to carry both hat-boxes in the other, she hurried down the stairs.

But when she was halfway down them, Barnes, who was waiting in the Hall, saw her and with an expression of surprise came to help her.

"You should have called me, Miss Alita," he said in a scolding voice, speaking with the familiarity of an old servant. "Are you going away?"

It was a question which Alita was asking herself, and without replying she put down the case at Barnes's feet and ran across the Hall to the Library.

Clint had just finished his letter and was propping it against the big silver ink-stand which graced her uncle's desk.

He rose as Alita entered and she ran across to him.

"Are you ready, my darling?" he enquired.

"There is... something I have to... ask you. There is... something I must... say," Alita said.

"What is worrying you?"

"It is just that I want to be... sure that you... understood what I... told you. You do... realise that my father's crime will... never be :.. forgiven? That people will look... embarrassed or... shocked when they know who I... am?"

She paused breathlessly before she added:

"Supposing... because of that... you cease to... love me and you are... sorry that you asked me to be your wife?"

Clint smiled very tenderly before he replied:

"I have already told you that I come from a family which has done all sorts of things that would make

154

the supercilious English raise their eye-brows and look down their noses. Personally, I could not care a damn!"

As he spoke, he saw the anxiety vanish from Alita's eyes, and then he said:

"When I cease to love you, as you suggest I might do, we will worry about it together. But I do not mind taking an odds-on bet that it is something that will never happen."

"How can you be . . . sure?"

"Because I love you," he answered. "I love you as I have never been in love before."

The radiance in her face was almost blinding, and then he said:

"I have told you to let the future take care of itself, or rather I will take care of it for you. But one thing is very sure—if the English do not want us, there are lots of other places that will."

He waited, with his eyes on her, and then he said:

"There is Ireland, for one, and France for another. I have always rather fancied the idea of boar-hunting, and if we want magnificent horses to ride, what could be more interesting than a trip to Hungary?"

"Oh, Clint!"

Alita could hardly breathe the words, and anything she was about to say he swept from her lips with his own, before he said:

"I have a number of other suggestions I could make, but let us go. I have a feeling that in a short time you will be hungry. What did you have for breakfast?"

She gave a little murmur that was half a laugh, for it was so like Clint to talk about something so mundane as breakfast when his kisses had made her feel that she was disembodied and would never want food again.

He smiled as if he knew the answer. Then, taking

her by the hand, he led her out of the Library, and into the Hall, where old Barnes was standing with the case and the hat-boxes.

"Will you be a-wanting these with you, Miss Alita?" he enquired. "You didn't tell me if you're going away."

"Yes, I am going away," Alita answered. "Will you tell His Grace that there is a letter for him on the desk in the Library?"

She held out her hand.

"Good-bye, Barnes."

The old Butler looked surprised, but he shook Alita's hand.

"Good-bye, Miss, and good luck, wherever you're going."

"Thank you," Alita said and smiled at him.

She walked to the front door and saw outside a Chaise drawn by a team of four superlative horses. Although she had seen them in the stables, she had never before seen them between the shafts.

She would have liked to stop and pat them, but she knew that Clint was eager to leave. She stepped into the Chaise, and the groom who was holding the horses' heads released them as he picked up the reins.

The groom helped Barnes put Alita's cases in behind, and then they were off, Clint driving with a skill that was comparable to the way he rode.

"Are we going in your private train?" Alita asked when they were halfway down the drive.

She looked back as she spoke. She had never believed that she would ever escape from the Castle, that she would not be incarcerated within its grey stone walls for the rest of her life.

"It is not my own," Clint answered, "although I have one in America. I have borrowed the one we are using now from a friend—the Earl of Derby. I think you will find it quite comfortable."

Alita gave a little sigh of excitement.

"I have always wanted to go in a private train. Papa told me about them many years ago, and I was so jealous when I heard that you had sent one for Nellie Farren and Miss Wadman."

"Is that the only thing which made you jealous?" Clint asked.

She moved a little closer to him, resisting an impulse to put her cheek against his shoulder.

"Miss Wadman is a...fellow-countryman," she said hesitatingly, "and so very...attractive."

"So is Nellie Farren," Clint said with a smile. "But I had fallen in love with a little thoroughbred who wanted grooming, and I found it hard to think of anything else!"

"I think I am...dreaming," Alita said, "and at any moment I am going to wake up to find that only the...horses care if I am alive or dead."

"As I have already said," Clint replied quietly, "that is all in the past. There are going to be a great many other interests for you in the future. More horses, of course; and most important, as far as I am concerned—me!"

Now Alita could not resist pressing her cheek against him with a little gesture that he found very moving.

"There is...nothing else but...you," she whispered.

* * *

Alita came slowly back to consciousness to find that she was riding, riding very smoothly and effortlessly. She thought she must be mounted on a strange horse that had a different stride from any she had known before.

Then she became aware that she was not riding but lying on a soft bed, and beneath her she heard the rumble of wheels.

Even as she was aware of where she was, two strong arms drew her close and a voice said:

"Are you awake, my precious?"

"Oh, darling Clint!"

She felt her love for him surge over her in a manner that made her reach blindly towards him, knowing that she must reassure herself that he was really there.

"The train has just started," he said. "It is still very early, but we want to arrive at Holyhead about noon."

Alita was listening, but at the same time her heart was singing to the voices of angels, because she was married.

She was Clint's wife and they were together in a private train that was carrying them away from everything that was depressing, unpleasant, and disturbing.

She still could not believe that her whole life had changed since yesterday morning, when she had found Clint waiting for her in the Drawing-Room of the Castle.

They had driven nearly three miles to the nearest station, and there, waiting in the siding, was a small private train that had an air of exclusiveness which proclaimed that it was used only by the very important and the very rich.

To Alita it was like being given a doll's-house, and she explored it excitedly.

She loved the flower-filled Drawing-Room carriage with its comfortable brocade-covered chairs, and the bed-room, which, she saw with a blush, was furnished with a brass bed that was big enough for two.

There was another room in the same coach, which Clint was to use as a dressing-room, and she found that the next carriage contained a single compartment for his valet and one for the maid he had engaged to look after her.

In another carriage was a kitchen and other compartments for the rest of the staff.

It was so fascinating; and even more exciting were the new clothes which Clint had provided her.

The maid told Alita that there were dozens of round-topped leather trunks in the guard's van.

"How could you think... how could you know ... that I... would ever... wear the clothes you had ... ordered for me?" she asked.

"I made up my mind to marry you," he answered, "and I could not really think of anything which would prevent me from getting my own way!"

"Supposing... after all the trouble and expense, you had... decided you did not... want me?"

"I told you that if you had committed a murder I would protect you, and seeing the way you looked, I thought it unlikely that you had robbed a bank, and I really could not imagine another crime in which you could be involved."

"You are not real!" Alita cried. "A man like you does not exist outside story-books."

"I will prove I am real, my darling," he replied, "but I think we should get married first!"

She blushed and hid her face against him.

Then she moved quickly away as the servants, wearing the livery of their noble master, brought in luncheon, and champagne, which Clint said was obligatory on such occasions.

The food was delicious, although it was hard for Alita to realise what she ate. She could only look into the blue eyes of the man who sat opposite her and feel herself thrill to every word he spoke.

Almost as soon as they had boarded the train she had changed into a gown which became her as much as the one she had worn last night.

It was not the conventional white that she should have worn as a bride, but instead it was the very soft blue of the mists hanging round the trees in the morning.

Barbara Cartland

It made her think of Clint riding towards her, making her feel as if he came from another world.

It was an exquisitely fashioned gown, swept into a bustle at the back, and with a close-fitting little jacket which revealed the soft curves of her figure and the tininess of her waist.

After her new maid had arranged her hair, she had gone into the Drawing-Room coach, and standing in front of him she had asked shyly:

"Do I ... look all right?"

There was a note in her voice and a look in her eyes which told him how important the question was.

"You look, my precious, very beautiful and even lovelier than I knew you could look!"

"You ... are sure?"

He rose and put his arms round her.

"You will grow very conceited," he said softly, "when I tell you over and over again that you are not only beautiful to look at but irresistible to touch and very exciting to kiss."

He looked at her for a long moment before he kissed her eyes, her cheeks, the corners of her mouth, and lastly as her breath came quickly between her parted lips he held them captive.

She was wearing a small feather hat with a short veil, and Alita knew when Clint gave her a bouquet of star-shaped white orchids that she not only looked like a bride but felt like one.

He had two presents for her, which he gave her before they left the train.

One was a huge sapphire engagement-ring surrounded by diamonds; the other, a two-strand necklace of perfect pearls.

He clasped the pearls round her neck and then kissed first her lips and then the little pulse that was beating excitedly just below her chin-line.

As he did so, she felt the quicksilver which had run through her when he had first kissed her dart through her whole body and end in a response from her own lips that made her feel as if they were united by a burning flame.

"I love ... you," she said. "How can I thank you ... except by saying over and over again: I ... love you."

"I will answer that question a little later," he replied, and his voice was very deep.

He kissed her again, passionately and compelingly, as if he could not help himself.

Then they stepped out onto a small wayside station which Alita knew was a halt used by the owner of some big Estate.

A carriage was waiting and they drove off towards a small village.

As Alita saw a Church ahead of them she looked at Clint and he explained:

"I thought that as essentially you belong to the country, you would prefer to be married in a country Church."

"It is not only what I would like," Alita said, "but I want to be ... alone with you ... without a lot of people staring at us."

"That is what I too want," he said. "The Earl of Derby arranged everything when I told him what I required. He also offered us the hospitality of his house, but I refused."

"I am so glad ... I just want to be with ... you," Alita said, and he kissed her hand as the carriage drew to a standstill.

The Church was massed with white flowers, many of them orchids to match Alita's bouquet. There were also huge bowls of Madonna lilies, which scented the whole building with their unforgettable fragrance.

The Parson was waiting for them at the altar and the Service was very quiet and very moving.

There was a solemn note in Clint's deep voice as he made his vows, a note which Alita thought she had never heard before, while her own voice sounded a little shy.

She prayed fervently that he would love her forever and that she should be exactly the wife he wanted.

The Parson blessed them, they signed the book in the Vestry, and then they left the Church and drove back the way they had come.

Alita held on tightly to Clint's hand.

"Am I... really your wife?" she asked. "Are you ... sure that ... nobody can say it is ... illegal, or stop me ... from belonging to you?"

There was just a touch of fear in her voice, because it was hard to believe that, after all she had suffered in thinking that no man would ever want her, she was now actually married.

"You are my wife," Clint said positively, "and the first thing I will teach you, my darling, is to believe that we will never lose each other and nothing shall ever come between us."

"That is ... all I want," she murmured.

She wanted to add that she was wildly in love with the most attractive man she had ever seen.

They reboarded the train, and when they were alone and Alita had taken off her hat and her little jacket, he kissed her until she felt as if he drew her heart from her body.

Then, as they sat together on a sofa at the end of the carriage, she said:

"When you ... first kissed me, I wanted to ... die, but now I want to live."

"That is why I am going to make sure you not only live but are happy," he answered. "You have, my adorable little wife, a lot of time to make up."

He kissed the finger that wore his ring and added:

"There is so much I have to teach you, and I know it will be more exciting than anything I have ever done before!"

THE RACE FOR LOVE

"More exciting than... winning a race?" Alita teased.

"That is what I have just done," he replied. "It has been a race for love, my precious, but I have passed the winning-post, and all you have to do now is to award me the prize."

"Is... that... me?" she asked shyly.

"Could it be anything else?... It is difficult to tell you, my sweet life, how much and how uncontrollably I want you."

The passion in the way he spoke and the fire in his eyes made her hide her face against him.

Then in a voice which he could barely hear she whispered:

"Teach... me, please teach... me to love you... as you want to be... loved."

* * *

Soon after dinner the train drew into a siding, so they could spend a quiet night.

Later, very much later, Alita said softly:

"I am... so happy... that I want to... cry."

"If you do I shall be angry," Clint replied. "There are to be no more tears, only smiles and laughter."

"I thought that was what you would want when I was at that marvellous party you gave for Nellie Farren."

"I want other things as well," he said, "but I can never allow you again to look so unhappy as you did when I first knew you."

"I did not... think you... noticed me."

"How could you imagine I would not notice anyone who rode as well as you?"

"It is a different thing from noticing my face and the real me."

"I soon found the real you!"

"I wish I had known," she said with a sigh. "I was so... convinced that... nobody would ever... notice me that I took no... trouble over myself."

"I am aware of that," Clint said in an amused voice.

Alita clung a little closer and then she turned her head to kiss his shoulder.

"How could... you have been so... clever as to realise that I could... look... very different?"

"I looked at you not only with my eyes," he answered, "but with my heart."

"Please always do... that," she begged, "and then your heart will tell you how... much I love you."

"Are you sure of that now?" he enquired.

"I did not know I could... feel as if we flew on wings high into the sky or dived deep down into the sea. It was so perfect... so divine."

"That is what I always want to make you feel."

Alita put her hand against his neck as if to pull him even closer to her, and then she said in a very small voice:

"There is... something I want to... say to... you."

"What is it?"

"I want to... make sure you... believe me."

"I have always believed what you have told me in the past."

"But what I have to say now... is something... different."

"Then tell me," he said.

She felt his lips against her hair, and because he was so gentle and so strong, so tender and yet so possessive, she felt herself thrill and her body quivered against him.

He drew in his breath, but, as if he knew that what she would say was important, he asked quietly:

"What is it you want to tell me?"

"I want you to... believe that I would... love you... just as I love you now... if you did not... have a penny in the... world."

The Race for Love

She paused before she went on, still in an intense little voice:

"It is ... wonderful to think of all the things we can ... have, horses, private trains, and houses anywhere we want, but ... none of that really ... matters. I love you ... because you are ... you, because you are the most marvellous ... wonderful man that ever ... existed. But I am so ... afraid that you do not ... understand that that is ... how I ... feel."

He turned towards her so that his heart was beating against hers, and his arms were round her and his lips very close to hers.

"I adore you, my lovely one, for what you have told me, but at the same time I knew it."

"How?"

"I knew it when I kissed you in the carriage."

"How did you ... know?"

"You gave me your soul on your lips, and I knew that was what I had always been seeking."

"Oh, Clint!"

"I have always," he went on, "longed to find a woman who would love me for myself and not be influenced by the fact that I could buy her anything she desired."

"You knew that I never ... dreamt you would ... give me ... anything."

In the faint light coming through the curtains which covered the windows of their carriage, Alita saw that he was smiling as he said:

"I had the greatest difficulty where you were concerned to get you to accept a new habit, and it required all my ingenuity to ensure that you had a trousseau."

"I still feel ... ashamed that you ... should have ... bought that."

"You have just told me," he answered, "that such things are unimportant, that it is only our love which counts."

"Only our... love," Alita repeated. "And I thought... when we were in the... dark and you... loved me... it did not matter how rich or how poor you were... no money could buy what you made me feel."

"You are my wife and that is what matters," Clint said. "My wife—mine! Tell me that is what you are—completely and absolutely!"

"You... know I... am yours."

He gave a little laugh. It was very tender.

"Mine, despite a great deal of opposition, but I told you I always get what I want in the end!"

"I know... that... now."

"And you shall never escape!"

Then he was kissing her, kissing her demandingly, fiercely, and passionately.

His hand was touching her body, making it quiver against him. He was the victor, the conqueror, the man who had won the race for love.

The quicksilver was running through Alita's body and the flames that rose in them both became a burning fire.

It was impossible to think of anything but love... love... love....

The rumble of the wheels beneath the carriage seemed to be echoing the same word over and over again:

Love... love... love!

SPECIAL OFFER: If you enjoyed this book and would like to have our catalog of over 1,400 other Bantam titles, just send your name and address and 50¢ (to help defray postage and handling costs) to: Catalog Department, Bantam Books, Inc., 414 East Golf Rd., Des Plaines, Ill. 60016.

ABOUT THE AUTHOR

BARBARA CARTLAND, the world's most famous romantic novelist, who is also an historian, playwright, lecturer, political speaker and television personality, has now written over 200 books. She has also had many historical works published and has written four autobiographies as well as the biographies of her mother and that of her brother Ronald Cartland, who was the first Member of Parliament to be killed in the last war. This book has a preface by Sir Winston Churchill. Barbara Cartland has sold 80 million books over the world, more than half of these in the U.S.A. She broke the world record in 1975 by writing twenty books, and her own record in 1976 with twenty-one. In private life, Barbara Cartland, who is a Dame of the Order of St. John of Jerusalem, has fought for better conditions and salaries for Midwives and Nurses. As President of the Royal College of Midwives (Hertfordshire Branch), she has been invested with the first Badge of Office ever given in Great Britain, which was subscribed to by the Midwives themselves. She has also championed-the-cause for old people and founded the first Romany Gypsy Camp in the world. Barbara Cartland is deeply interested in Vitamin Therapy and is President of the British National Association for Health.

Deb 270-8631

Barbara Cartland

The world's bestselling author of romantic fiction. Her stories are always captivating tales of intrigue, adventure and love.

☐	11270	THE LOVE PIRATE	$1.50
☐	11271	THE TEMPTATION OF TORILLA	$1.50
☐	11372	LOVE AND THE LOATHSOME LEOPARD	$1.50
☐	11410	THE NAKED BATTLE	$1.50
☐	11512	THE HELL-CAT AND THE KING	$1.50
☐	11537	NO ESCAPE FROM LOVE	$1.50
☐	11580	THE CASTLE MADE FOR LOVE	$1.50
☐	11579	THE SIGN OF LOVE	$1.50
☐	11595	THE SAINT AND THE SINNER	$1.50
☐	11649	A FUGITIVE FROM LOVE	$1.50
☐	11797	THE TWISTS AND TURNS OF LOVE	$1.50
☐	11801	THE PROBLEMS OF LOVE	$1.50
☐	11751	LOVE LEAVES AT MIDNIGHT	$1.50
☐	11882	MAGIC OR MIRAGE	$1.50
☐	10712	LOVE LOCKED IN	$1.50
☐	11959	LORD RAVENSCAR'S REVENGE	$1.50

Buy them at your local bookstore or use this handy coupon:

Bantam Books, Inc., Dept. BC, 414 East Golf Road, Des Plaines, Ill. 60016

Please send me the books I have checked above. I am enclosing $_____ (please add 50¢ to cover postage and handling). Send check or money order—no cash or C.O.D.'s please.

Mr/Mrs/Miss_____

Address_____

City_____ State/Zip_____

BC2—7/78

Please allow four weeks for delivery. This offer expires 1/79.